Katie O'Connor

Christmas
in
Berry Cove

A
*Romantic
Short Story
Collection*

Christmas

in

Berry Cove

Katie O'Connor

* Christmas in Berry Cove *

*A Romantic Short Story Collection *

Published November 2025 by Snarky Heart Press and Katie O'Connor.

(katieohwrites.com)

ISBN: 978-1-997548-14-0 Ebook

ISBN: 978-1-997548-15-7 Alternate Ebook

ISBN: 978-1-997548-16-4 Print

ISBN: 978-1-997548-17-1 Alternate Print Print

Copyediting by Terri St. Clair

·❤·❤·❤·❤·❤·

Dear Readers:

This collection of five short stories began as a single limited edition paper copy to be mailed out to my fans as a Christmas gift. Year one went great. Year two, I got distracted, and the story was released late. Year three? I was ready in advance, but Canada Post was on strike. That's when I gave up on the idea of mailing and altered my plan.

Since the first five stories were already written, I've decided to put them together into a collection. Christmas in Berry Cove is the result of that decision. I must warn you, the heat level varies by couple. Some couples are just more eager to hop into bed, I guess. The stories range from sweet to steamy, but they are all closed door.

I hope you love spending Christmas in Berry Cove.

And be sure to watch for the next story, coming soon. Santa willing, and fingers crossed.

Katie

Dedication

This one is for Jules, Jennifer, Brian,
and the rest of the crew at Advanced Dental.
Thanks for the great care and support.
May you all flourish in love and caring.

♥ · ♥ · ♥ · ♥ · ♥

Love in Time for Christmas

·♥·♥·♥·♥·♥·

Chapter One

J oyous Christmas carols rang out from speakers strung outside local shops as Trudy Marshall hurried down Main Street in her hometown of Berry Cove. With only days until Christmas, there was something magical in the air. It was more than the Christmas spirit. There was joy and a sense of blessings to come. Everyone was smiling at each other and calling out cheerful greetings. It was like she'd stumbled into a holiday romance movie. Only better.

The air was brisk, starting to drop toward real winter cold. The speakers' sound faded as she approached a group of singers in Dickensian costumes serenading passersby on a street corner. A gray-bearded man with sparkling eyes, wearing an old-fashioned waistcoat and top hat, led them in chorus. She'd almost swear he winked at her as she passed.

The music filled her heart with joy, and a smile crept over her face. Despite her lack of time to enjoy the moment, this was holiday bliss, and her favorite time of year.

Though she wanted to listen, she had just a short time to make it to the toy store before it closed. If she didn't get there on time, she'd probably miss her only chance to get her nephew Tyrone the fabulous Lego kit he was begging for. Her sister had scoured Calgary toy shops and the internet in vain. Trudy had been talking to the postmistress, who mentioned the Harry Potter set by name.

She rushed along, cradling the coffee she'd purchased on her way to the post office. She didn't want to spill one precious drop. She needed every mouthful to fuel her late-night writing. By day, she was the receptionist at Berry Cove's town office. By night, she penned steamy romances and a blog about spicing up your love life...not that she had a love life right now, and if she didn't finish her latest novel by next week, she'd miss her deadline, for the fourth time, and her editor would be irate. She could lose her contract over this.

She didn't know why the words refused to come. After writing seventy-two books, she should have it down pat. In fact, if you'd have asked her six months ago, she'd have told you she could write in her sleep. Maybe her imagination was drying up along with her love life.

She paused at the first of two traffic lights between her and the toy store. She was tempted to jaywalk, but the chief of police was sitting in his cruiser on the opposite side of the street. No sense risking a ticket. She stomped her feet to keep them warm. She looked down in dismay as slush splashed onto the toes of her thin dressy boots. She knew better than to wear pretty shoes when snow was scheduled, and now it was coming down by the bucketful.

Huge lacy flakes whirled on the light breeze before drifting down and piling up. Thank heaven there wasn't much wind or she'd be half frozen to death. It was December first, and she'd been avoiding winter clothing. That ended here...well, it ended when she got home and dug her winter gear out of the closet. She snuggled deeper into her jacket, trying to protect herself from the icy breeze.

Cars splashed past, some slowing, some seeming bent on soaking everyone who lined the quaint sidewalks along Main Street, Berry Cove. She eased back half a step lest someone splash her tan pants and ruin them. The light going the other direction changed to yellow. She peered left and right in preparation to cross.

A rusty Ford pickup careened down the street, weaving wildly, swerving into the other lane and nearly back onto the sidewalk. The driver was a menace. He veered left, then back right, straight toward her.

"Crap!" She jumped back out of his path and slammed into something solid. Her coffee flew from her hand, up into the air, and over her shoulder.

"What the…?" a deep male voice behind her cried out in surprise. *Oh no!*

Trudy whirled round and bumped into a solid wall of flesh. Dripping wet flesh, covered in a coffee-soaked, once white dress shirt. "I'm so sorry." She looked up and up into the scowling face of the man who dumped her five years ago. Maxim Langtree. Shoot. Of all the people…

Her gaze travelled to emerald eyes below a pinched brow. She was struck mute by their deep fire. His hands gripped her arms, keeping her from teetering over on her slender heels.

"Are you okay?" His frown deepened then morphed into an enormous smile. "Trudy!" He crushed her into a hug. "It's been way too long."

"Maxim, sorry, I didn't mean to drench you," she blathered. She wanted to sink into the slush and melt away.

"I'm not sorry. I've been looking all over town for you." The frown eased. He waved at the front of his formerly white dress shirt and coffee coated suit jacket. "I assume this belonged to you?"

"Yes. Oh, I'm so sorry, Max." Heat rose in her face as she stared at his chest. His shirt clung to his muscles like a lover. Like she used to do. Oh, she missed those days.

Stop! You're over him.

"Send the dry-cleaning bill to City Hall, and I'll reimburse you. I swear." She held up her fingers in a Girl Guide salute. His eyes widened, and he grinned.

"I really will pay to have that cleaned. Send the bill in my name. Gotta run."

She'd love to talk to him, except just looking at his familiar face made her heart ache. They'd been good together until he left her for his career.

She hurried across the street, barely making it before the light changed to red. Solid footsteps sounded behind her. She risked a glance toward the sound. Max was striding along in the same direction.

She slipped into the toy store and made a beeline for the Lego section, and scanned the shelves. Nothing. It wasn't there! She sighed and stomped her foot. She muttered under her breath, "This sucks."

"That sounds serious."

She turned to Max, who must have followed her inside. "It is. I really needed a kit for my nephew. I thought it was here. I don't know what to do now." She wasn't one to give in to any old whim by her nephew, but he'd had a tough year, and she wanted to make his Christmas extra special.

"Let me help you look. What do you need?" His smile and offer slipped right into her heart.

She explained the Harry Potter kit.

"Okay, I'm on it. If it's here, I'll find it for you." He went to the other end of the aisle and started shifting boxes. She watched him stretch to the top shelf and rearrange kits. He was still fit and gorgeous with his short dark beard and his flashing green eyes. She did love green eyes. And his height still made her swoon.

She started at the bottom on the opposite end of the aisle and dug through every package. Ten minutes later, they were bumping shoulders in the middle. He smelled incredible. Beyond the scent of her mocha was something spicy and minty. She inhaled deeply. So delicious.

He squatted down as she reached higher to shift another kit. She placed one hand on his shoulder for support. *Oh yeah, solid as a rock.*

"Oh! Is this it?" He held up a kit and looked up at her, an enormous smile stretched across his cheeks. She stared into his eyes; the kit entirely forgotten. All she could think about was how much she had loved him, before...

"Trudy?" His smile was slightly mocking and entirely endearing.

She shook her head. "Um. Yeah. Sorry. I got distracted for a second." He shook the package in excitement, and she glanced at it. "Yes! Oh, it is the one I need. Thank you so much."

He stood and passed her the kit. Impulsively, she flung her arms around him in a hug. *Lord, he's rock-hard and she just wanted to melt into him.* She jumped back; her face flooded with heat. "I'm so sorry. I was just so excited."

"No problem." His low laugh rumbled across her skin and into her heart.

His wink went straight to her heart. All her old feelings rushed forward. Love, disappointment, longing, lust, love. She needed to pull herself together.

"You can make it up to me by buying me a coffee." He paused. "And by not spilling it on me."

"Funny." She raised a brow at him. His teasing was still adorable. "As soon as I pay for this kit, I'm all over coffee. I owe you big time. For the toy, and for the spillage."

·❤· ❤· ❤· ❤· ❤·

Chapter Two

Maxim smiled at Trudy as they took their seats in Annie's Café amid a myriad of tinsel, bells, and holiday greenery. She was as beautiful as she was five years ago. Maybe more so. She'd gained a few curves, and the years had only made her prettier. Her blonde hair was short and spiked up, her green eyes sparkling with life and happiness. She looked like a Christmas sprite.

He'd seen her exit the town office and had delayed his visit to the mayor to follow her. It was astounding how she'd drawn him like a rope pulling right on his heart. He'd missed her every second of every day when they'd been apart. Seeing her again was pure heaven. Except for the guilt of leaving her.

"What brings you back to Berry Cove?" She sipped her mint hot cocoa. A small drop of whipped cream stuck to her lip, and she licked it off.

He swallowed hard. She was too enticing, and her impact hadn't lessened one bit.

"Work. I bought a business here. I was on my way to see the mayor when I saw you."

She blinked in confusion. "If you were going to see the mayor, how did you end up in the toy store?"

"I thought we could talk." His heart knew her. She was the love he was looking for, the one he'd let go in a moment of idiocy, and he wanted her back. She was the real reason he'd returned to Berry Cove.

"Talk about what?"

He loved how she didn't put up with partial answers. "I decided you were a Christmas miracle, sent straight to me." He shrugged, "I was headed to City Hall, the carolers were playing, *It's Beginning To Look a Lot Like Christmas*. I spotted you just when the lyrics said, *"The prettiest sight you'll see."* It felt like...destiny."

Her eyes went wide and darted back and forth. She leaned toward him like she was going to impart a secret. He slid forward until their faces were only inches apart. She licked her lip nervously. "When I turned around and you were there, I felt the same thing. A little zing jolted through my heart," she confessed with a sweet blush.

Her laugh was like angel bells. "Scared the ever-loving crap out of me. Because...instant attraction? After what you did to me? It doesn't happen."

"I'd like to talk about that. I have a few things to say, to apologize for."

Indecision danced across her face. He saw a no, a yes, and something that looked distinctly like *this is a bad idea*. He pulled back and picked up his orange spice tea, feigning nonchalance, and waited, fear in his heart. He couldn't mess this up again.

"You know what? I'm not sure about that discussion, but I'd like to catch up." She grinned. "Want to go to the craft fair? I've got shopping to do."

Ah. A test. Because men hate shopping. She wasn't getting rid of him that easily. "I'm okay with that. I need a gift for my mom and my sister." He slipped his family in because she'd always been close to them. She still visited his family, just never when he was home to visit.

The craft market was packed. People clustered around all the vendors. The enticing scents of mini-donuts lingered in the air along with cranberry-apple cider and fresh hot coffee. He followed Trudy as she squished herself between smiling patrons and inched up to the fudge table.

"Franny, I need a fix." She laughed. "Rocky road, maple, cranberry-orange, and pecan, please."

"Is that to go, or are you eating it here?" Franny teased.

"Both?" They laughed together, and Max couldn't help but join in. Trudy was the sunniest, most easy-going person he knew.

"Do you want anything, Max?" Trudy asked.

"I'll take one of those flavor packs, to go. On my bill, not Trudy's," he said to Franny.

She offered a tray of samples, and Trudy devoured four immediately before turning to him. "You know the sampler has sixteen flavors, right?"

"I do. I like fudge, so does my sister. And I'm sort of seeing this woman who likes it too. I re-met her today, and I'm trying to impress her."

"Indeed?" She grinned and lifted one eyebrow skeptically. "How's that going?"

"I'll let you know as soon as I know. It looks good so far." He couldn't resist the blatant *Top Gun* rip-off. They'd watched the old movie together a dozen times. He loved the jets. She adored the romance.

Her laugh rang out again, and people around them smiled at her joy. His heart tripped, and he couldn't stop returning her jubilant expression. This was the most fun he'd had in years, come to think of it, probably, since he left her. Coming back to Berry Cove was the best decision he'd ever made.

They wandered up and down the rows, chatting with one another and talking to vendors. He wanted to start apologizing or start explaining why he'd cut and run. More importantly, he wanted to talk about why he was back. It was hard to push the issue in public.

Trudy picked up a blue and white flannel shirt and a pair of men's gloves. He wondered who they were for. Did he have competition?

"Tell me, Trudy, are you single, married, dating, engaged?" He held his breath waiting for an answer.

"Currently unattached in all ways. How about you? I mean, aside from your mystery woman."

"Single. Completely. My mystery woman is you."

She reared back slightly in response to his declaration. He hadn't meant to spring it on her, but he didn't want her to think he was a cheater. She needed to know he was fully into her and no one else. He'd messed up with her once; and he sure as heck wasn't going to do that again. "Single for a very long time. I haven't dated in over two years."

· ♥ · ♥ · ♥ · ♥ · ♥ ·

Chapter Three

T hey shopped until Trudy wanted to drop. She was laden down with bags and starting to tire. "I think I need a rest. What time is it?"

Max glanced at his Rolex. "Seven-thirty. Holy cow. I can't believe we've spent nearly three hours in the market. Where did the time go? Time flies when you're having fun, I guess." He didn't seem at all upset.

"I think I need food. Something more substantial than fudge and mini-donuts, though they were delicious. Dinner?"

"Yes, please. Right after we visit Santa," he suggested.

"You want to sit on Santa's knee?" She giggled. "Sure, why not. You first. Then I'll go...if you don't squish him."

They joined the short queue at Santa's village, and it was Max's turn before they knew it. He sat on a stool next to the familiar-looking, bearded old man, and they chatted in whispers for a long time, each of them sneaking glances at Trudy. She wondered what all the secrecy was about. Then, it was her turn.

The man sitting on the black leather and silver throne was the most realistic Santa impersonator she'd ever seen. His beard was absolutely real and curled delightfully. His suit was crushed red velvet with what seemed to be actual fur trim. His round little silver glasses framed bright blue laughing eyes. She could almost swear she'd seen him before.

"Good evening, Trudy," he said when she settled beside him.

"Max told you my name." He couldn't fool her.

"Actually, no. I've known both you and Max for years, decades. Though I have known Max for a bit longer than I've known you."

It was easy to guess people's ages. She wasn't biting on that one. She'd let the old man have his fun. It was sweet how he kept fully in Santa character.

"You've always been a good girl and a true believer in the spirit of the season. That's why I'm going to grant you an extra special Christmas wish this year. Lean close, Trudy, and tell me what you want for Christmas."

"Hm. I think I'd like a new winter jacket. Mine's getting old. Maybe something in a deep red wool." She smiled. She'd been eyeing the jacket she described for months.

"Ho ho ho." His laugh rang loudly, startling her. "Don't be silly. Don't waste the ultimate wish on material things. Lean close and tell me what you *really* want this year."

Despite this being all in fun, she couldn't help confessing her deepest desire. "Santa, I need someone who understands me, someone who loves me, and someone who needs me. I need my one true love. A love like you and Mrs. Claus share. Eternal love with my soul mate." Heat filled her face, and she couldn't help but glance at Max.

"Is that how it is?" Santa whispered with a less-than-discreet nod at Max.

She blushed and giggled. "Maybe. But we have a past. He left me. He hurt me. Sure, he's handsome and kinder than he was, but I really don't know him anymore. He seems different. There were certainly sparks when we re-met, and he didn't get mad when I pitched hot coffee on his chest. That's good, right?"

"That's excellent. I'll tell you what. I'll see what I can do for you this year. Keep believing, Trudy. Remember that people change.

Don't forget that this is the time of love and forgiveness. Wishes do come true, especially with a little Santa magic." He winked, and for a fraction of a second, she was certain his eyes glittered with magic. She shook off the fanciful thought.

"Thanks, Santa. Merry Christmas." She rose and shook his hand. "It was nice meeting you. You're the most realistic Santa I've ever seen."

"That's because I'm the real deal. No stand-ins or fakes here. Ho ho ho."

In that moment, right there, in the market, she believed him. She joined Max, who was waiting patiently near the reindeer petting zoo.

"That was fun!" She knew her face was glowing.

"It was. He was awesome. Now, let me take you to dinner. I just got us into Cupid's on a cancellation." Cupid's was Berry Cove's premier and most romantic restaurant.

"Wow. That's a spot of luck. I haven't been there for years. Am I okay the way I am, or do I need to change?" She looked down at her outfit. Pretty blouse and sweater, and a knee-length skirt atop her tall dress boots. She looked professional, but not at all date-like. Max, on the other hand, looked one hundred percent date-ready, even with coffee stains.

He was so different from the pencil-thin youth who had abandoned her for his career. He'd matured and filled out. He was patient, and his smile still stole the breath from her chest.

·♥·♥·♥·♥·♥·

Chapter Four

C upid's was as intimate and romantic as Max had heard. It was the perfect place for an apology. A long overdue apology. The maître d' seated them at a secluded table hidden behind greenery and low walls.

The wine he'd asked for was ready, and the pre-ordered appetizers arrived moments after it was poured. He'd selected all her favorites. A large mixed plate including potato skins, deep-fried mozza sticks, calamari, and bruschetta. He was out to impress. Not by spending money, but by showing her that he knew her and remembered what she liked.

"How are you enjoying working for the town of Berry Cove?"

"You know what? I love it." Her smile was enormous. "I'm sure you remember me speaking about my best friend, Julia. She's the mayor, and it's great working for her. I'm putting my business degree to work, just not the way I thought I would. When you walked and left me alone, I took some time off work and came home to heal. Mom and Dad were very supportive. Julia was great." She sipped her wine.

Julia's receptionist went into labor before they finished hiring someone new, and I stepped in to help out. I loved the small-town atmosphere and working with people I know. I just ended up staying. I'm happier here than I was in the city."

She didn't add, with you, but he heard it in her voice.

"I'm glad. My folks keep me updated on what you're doing," he confessed. No secrets between them this time around.

"And mine about you, too. I heard you sold your software company for a mint. Congratulations. But why are you back?" Her voice held curiosity and well-deserved accusation.

"The truth?" She nodded, so he continued as she munched on a potato skin. "I came for you."

She laughed, and a bit of potato flew out of her mouth before she managed to cover it. She calmed down, swallowed, and wrinkled her nose at him. "That's rich."

"That's the truth." He clasped her hands in his, relieved when she didn't pull away. "I screwed up. I thought I couldn't be a success with a woman tying me down. I was wrong. Dead wrong. Dinosaur dead wrong. You were my support, my confidant, my shield. But most of all, you were my heart. I died when I left."

"And yet you stayed away." She stopped eating and frowned at the food. "It's easy to say those pretty words." Trudy obviously didn't believe him. "Easy to make up later, after your needs change. If you needed me so badly, why did you stay away? You could have called. Or texted."

"Because I was pinned to my foolish pride." He squeezed her hands lightly, like he was imploring her to believe. "I threw everything into my work. I became a success, and it was the hollowest victory in my life. Worse than when I got caught cheating on the math finals in grade twelve. Hollow and empty. I was a shell of a man. Kind of like Scrooge, or the Grinch. Loveless."

He inhaled deeply and chugged half his wine for courage. "It got worse over the years. The longer I was without you, the more I needed you. That's when I knew what I had to do."

"And what's that?" She should be mad that he'd dumped her and had been too cowardly to come back, but part of her understood. She'd been too afraid to chase him. Maybe if she had gone after him instead of running home, they might have found common ground and made up.

"I had to come back and find you, and grovel because I am nothing without you. You've been my heart and soul since we were fifteen. At twenty, I became an idiot and left you. I wasted nearly a decade running from my feelings. Then, it took a couple more to admit what I needed. Now, I'm back, and I'm not giving up on you, on me, on us."

Her heart pattered wildly. She'd dreamt of this for years. She'd dated other men, but none could fill the hole in her heart. The one he'd left when he pulled himself away.

"Trudy Marshall, you are my heart and soul. I love you with every breath in my body. I loved you then, I love you now. I never stopped." He slid out of his chair and onto one knee. He flipped open a green velvet box. A sparkling red stone sat in a rose-shaped setting. "I came back for you, for my heart. Will you give me another chance?"

She swallowed. She didn't know what to say. She wanted this, but there was so much unresolved between them. Finally, she squeaked out, "I don't know you anymore; I can't marry you." Her heart squeezed in pain.

"I'm not asking you to marry me. This is a promise ring. I promise to love you and care for you. I promise to be honest and to do right by you. I promise that you are my heart, and I promise I won't run again. Trudy, will you go steady with me? Please."

The naked entreaty in his voice swept away all the pain of their broken past. Love rushed in.

Her heart tripped happily; her pulse thrummed. A sense of peaceful joy washed over her. The moment was magical.

"Yes, Maxim Langtree, I will."

She stood and pulled him to his feet. "And I promise to keep loving you as I've loved you all these years."

Across the room, a gray-bearded man in a stylish top hat watched the interaction. His eyes misted with happy tears. He'd worked hard on this pair; they'd been stubborn. Maxim and Trudy weren't together yet, but Christmas magic and their undying love would do the trick.

Next year, he'd visit again and plant the idea that they needed to start their family. He put a finger to his nose and disappeared in a puff of magic.

· ♥ · ♥ · ♥ · ♥ · ♥ ·

The Mayor's Christmas Love

·♥·♥·♥·♥·♥·

Chapter One

S low dance music drifted around her as Julia looked over the crowd at her best friend's wedding reception. The community center's doors were propped wide open to let the warm, late September air in. The reception hall was bedecked in bright fall foliage. Mums, sunflowers, and tons of greenery. Doorways were hung with Gerbera daisies and ferns. It was a garden paradise.

She loved the fall theme, but her heart swelled at the idea of a Christmas wedding. It had been her secret dream for as long as she could remember. The dream she'd never shared with anyone, not even her closest friends, because it would never happen. There wasn't a man on earth who could overlook her past and her dedication to her job.

Tonight's celebration was for her friends, Trudy and Max, who had reconnected last Christmas after years apart. Now, less than a year later, they were tying the knot. The outdoor ceremony had been beautiful despite the chill in the air.

She whispered thanks that Trudy chose lovely dresses and faux fur wraps for her attendants. She could have picked something all froufrou and silly; instead, the dress was elegant, with just a hint of sexy. Perfect for a woman who was also the mayor.

Julia loved her little town. She'd grown up here in Berry Cove and had jumped into the mayoral race when the previous mayor had died suddenly. Surprisingly, only a few people had held her unusual family background against her, and she'd won by a landslide.

She smiled as she studied the guests. She knew most of them and loved having her hand in every little thing happening in town. Not because she was a control freak, more because she loved Berry Cove with every fiber of her being. This town had supported her and cared for her when her grandmother hadn't. She loved Berry Cove like a spouse. Her girlfriends teased her about being married to her work. She'd like to deny it, but she lived for her job.

The crowd parted to reveal a man sitting alone in the far corner, a frown twisting his face as he watched the revelers. Aside from his glower, he was gorgeous. His hair was a deep auburn, with more than a few hints of red. His beard was short and neat. Even sitting, he looked tall and broad-shouldered. Just her type of guy, if she was looking. Only why was he sitting alone? He wasn't even enjoying the cheerful dance music.

"As mayor of Berry Cove, it is your sworn duty to make him feel welcome," she whispered to herself. Yup, that's why she was going over, not because even frowning, he drew her like a magnet.

His glance skimmed past her and flashed back. The corners of his mouth lifted, and his eyes widened. *Holy smoking snow plows, he was hot.*

Eyes locked with his, she walked slowly toward him, loving the tip-tap of her delicate heels on the marble floor of the Banff Room of the Berry Cove Inn.

She reached his table and thrust out her hand. "Hi. I'm Julia Abrams. You must be friends with the groom. Welcome to Berry Cove." He rose and took her hand in his. His palm was warm, his handshake firm. Heat raced up her arm and coursed through her. She stifled a gasp. *Wow! He packed a punch.*

"Neil Buch. Nice to meet you, Julia. Max and I went to university together. We shared a dorm room for a year. How do you know the bride and groom?" He gestured to the chair beside his. "Please. Join me." His face glowed with a welcoming smile.

"I've known them for years. Trudy and I go way back. She's my bestie." She wasn't sure what to say next. She was uncharacteristically speechless. She was never without something to say. Her friends relied on her to keep conversations going when they ran flat. Right now, all she could do was stare into Neil's bright blue eyes.

Finally, coherent thought returned. "What do you do for a living, Neil?" It wasn't brilliant, but at least she wasn't just staring. Okay, she was staring, but she was talking too.

"I'm between jobs right now." He shrugged as if being unemployed didn't matter. With the cut of his expensive suit, she'd have thought he'd be more concerned. Maybe he'd rented it.

"That's too bad. I hope you find something soon."

"Oh, I'm sure something will show up. I'm not in a rush because I'm looking for a new place to call home. Toronto is too busy, though I enjoyed my time there."

She filed the small detail of his former home away for safekeeping. A new place to live was in her conversational wheelhouse. "You won't find a better place to live than Berry Cove. We're quiet but still have all the amenities you need. We're friendly and helpful. We celebrate all the seasons with festivals and carnivals. We've got a rink for skating, a bowling alley, a curling rink, and a gym. A ton of great places to eat. There's the lake, of course. Swimming, boating, ice fishing, and snowmobiling. We've got great snowshoe trails that double as walking trails in the summer. You'd never be bored." She couldn't help but praise the town she adored.

Neil quirked one eyebrow. "Are you the town's PR manager?"

She laughed. "Um. Actually, I'm the mayor." She shrugged. "I love this town. There isn't a better place to live. You should hang around after the wedding and check out all Berry Cove has to offer. There are plenty of businesses looking for help."

"I might do that. Right now, I'm staying in Maxim's guest house. It's quite cozy."

She'd seen that guest house. It was bigger than her apartment. Three bedrooms, an office, three baths. There was a glorious stone fireplace inside, and a brick fire pit outside. It even had a sauna and hot tub. Quite the place to stay when you were out of work.

Being unemployed and living at his friend's house didn't leave a great impression. But he was friends with Maxim and Trudy, which gave him some credit. Max ran his own business; maybe he'd hire Neil.

"Would you like a drink?" Neil asked. "I was just debating getting another."

"That would be nice. Why don't I come with you? I can introduce you around as we go." They strolled around the perimeter of the dance floor rather than dodging whirling dancers. How was it that the *Bunny Hop* and the *Macarena* were still popular at weddings, even here in country music central? She introduced him to her assistant, the office manager, and a few couples she knew before they arrived at the bar.

"What will you have?" he asked, waving his hand toward the bar.

"I'll have a virgin pina colada." She laughed when his eyebrows shot up into his hairline.

"I'm sorry. I didn't realize you don't drink. I apologize."

"No apology necessary. I do drink. I'm in a 5K race tomorrow, and I don't want to show up dehydrated. Of course, all the sugary juice in that isn't the best option either. But this is a celebration. My best friend got married!"

He ordered their drinks and turned his attention back to her. "Do you mean the Fall Foliage Fly? I entered too. It's a great way to raise money for the food bank. I was actually surprised to find out there are needy people here."

The compassion in his voice said he didn't mean to sound disparaging, though some might have taken it that way.

"Unfortunately, times are tough, and there are quite a few who need a helping hand. With Thanksgiving and Christmas both on the horizon, we're prepping ahead."

"I love that. I try to be generous with charities and pitch in when I can. Especially this time of year when need is so high."

Oh, sweet heaven. She loved a charitable man. Especially a good-looking one with manners. She picked up her beverage and took a sip. Pineapple and coconut flooded her taste buds. "Oh, this is good." She was a sucker for anything sweet, which was why running and kickboxing were part of her daily routine.

They stepped aside to make room at the bar for the people behind them. Moving left, they found a space by the wall and stood admiring the dancers undulating on the floor with various degrees of talent. Watching some of them, she didn't feel so bad about her lack of skill. They finished their drinks and placed their glasses in a nearby bin.

"Do you dance?" Neil asked when the fast song morphed into a slower number.

"I love dancing. Except I suck. I've got two left feet." She turned and grinned at him. "Are you offering?"

He bowed low and held out his hand. "My lady, would you care to take a turn about the floor?"

She placed her hand in his. "I would be delighted," she quipped back, meaning every word with a wholeheartedness she could barely contain. While she was respected in Berry Cove, smart people knew that if they valued their toes, they shouldn't ask her to dance. She put her hand on his elbow and let him lead her onto the floor. She stepped into his loose embrace and grimaced. "Sorry for the damage I'm going to do to your toes."

"You'll be fine. Nobody is that bad." He flashed her a heart-stopping wink, and she stumbled. He smirked. "Or maybe they are. Let's do this." He led her in a slow waltz. An actual waltz, not just hugging and foot shuffling. It brought back memories of the dance unit of high school gym class when nobody wanted to be her partner.

She did well for the first twenty-one steps. Then she stepped on his left foot. "Sorry."

"Relax, Julia, you're too tense. Take a deep breath and follow my lead."

She immediately stepped on his right foot, then stumbled forward, crushing their chests together. *Oh, he's solid muscle.* Heat flooded her face. "I'm sorry." She stared down at her toes, trying to get them to move in unison with his. She stepped on his toe again, and he stopped moving. She looked up to apologize.

"Julia, relax. You can't dance staring at your toes." His voice was kind. He stepped back from her. "This is the basic move." He moved his feet in a simple box pattern. "Follow me." She looked down at her feet. "Eyes up here," he teased.

"O-kay." She inhaled a steadying breath and was hit with his soapy manly scent. Definitely not steady. She looked up, and her eyes met his. He didn't look upset. He seemed...compassionate. "Lead on."

"Make the box. That's all we'll do until you get it." He placed his hands on her waist.

She wasn't a large woman, nor was she tiny, but his wide hands and long fingers made her feel delicate and small. She tried and tried to get the box. After a few moments, the unfamiliar song morphed into the band's version of Michael Bublé's *When I Fall in Love*. One of her favorite songs, though she'd deny it if asked. She hummed along and relaxed into his heady embrace.

·♥·♥·♥·♥·♥·

Chapter Two

Neil had been watching Julia for hours—right from the minute she stepped through the church's doors, preceding Trudy up the aisle until. He's stayed fascinated until she came and introduced herself.

There wasn't a lecherous bone in his body, but that dress should be illegal for the way it highlighted her curves. Her beautiful red hair was up in some fancy updo with a few loose tendrils. He wanted to see that glorious mass spilling down her back.

During the dinner, she'd been at the head table. She ate delicately but eagerly. It seemed ridiculous that he noticed she'd cleared her plate, but he was a man of details. Being aware of everything going on around him was how he'd built his software company into a gaming empire. Buch Games had served him well. Well enough that he'd sold it for an obscene amount of money, allowing him to retire at thirty-five. Oh, he certainly wouldn't stay retired, but he had no intention of building another enormous empire. He wanted something small, with more human contact. All that was beside the point because, at the moment, all he wanted to think about was the beautiful woman dancing in his arms.

She wasn't as bad at dancing as she thought she was. Perhaps her other partners had lacked the skills to guide her. They danced dozens of songs before, unable to resist, he edged her hand to his shoulder and slipped his hand to the sweet curve of her waist. "You don't mind dancing a bit closer, do you?"

"Um. No. It's okay." She sounded a bit breathless.

"Do you need to take a break?" He hoped not.

"Oh, no!" She blushed. "I'm good. You're a great dancer." Her smile nearly overheated him. She had pretty eyes and delicious curves a man could love.

"You're a pretty good dancer yourself." Her light laugh made him smile. He did enjoy a woman with the ability to laugh at herself. Especially a beautiful one. He'd love to pull her flush against his body, but she was the mayor and had a reputation to uphold. He couldn't, wouldn't, ignore her needs. She was passionate about this town, and he respected that.

People smiled as they danced past, though he doubted Julia noticed. Her eyes were closed, and she kept leaning toward him. If she didn't quit, he was going to do something they'd both regret and pull her closer than two strangers should ever dance. He wasn't a prude, but it was much too soon for a public display of affection.

She leaned against him. He took exactly three seconds to memorize the feeling of her warm curves against him before he stepped back. "Hey, I could use a drink. How about you?"

She blinked up at him, her eyes half-lidded and entirely too sexy. She cleared her throat and looked disappointed, though she nodded.

"More dancing later. I don't think either of us wants to be dehydrated for the race tomorrow, even if it is a fun run."

Her shoulders heaved in a sigh. "I suppose you're right."

He took her hand and led her back to the bar, where bottles of water sat in a tub of ice.

"Where is everyone?" She stopped and looked around the hall. "Everyone is gone." Only a few couples remained on the dance floor.

"That's it for us, folks. Enjoy your evening," the band's lead singer announced.

"Wow, is it that late? I had no idea," she stared at him, a confused wrinkle forming on her brow.

"Apparently. I was so distracted by you that I didn't notice the time. Can I drive you home?" He cracked open a water bottle and handed it to her.

"Um. I only live two blocks away. I'll just walk. But thanks."

It was much too early to part from her. He wanted to talk with her a while longer. "Can I walk you home?" He quirked one eyebrow in question. "I promise not to take advantage of you."

"And if I want to take advantage of you?" she quipped, her cheeks pinkening.

"As a gentleman, I'd be forced to permit you to have your way with me." He was playing along, joking, though he wouldn't turn her down.

"In that case, we'd better go to your place. I have nosy neighbors, and you have a private driveway."

He stared at her for a full minute, trying to decide if she was serious. He swallowed hard and gulped half his water, trying to compose himself. His heart thundered, and his body temperature skyrocketed. "Your wish is my command. Do you have anything to gather before we go?"

"Just my wrap. It's at the head table."

"No wallet or purse?" he asked as they strolled hand in hand to her seat.

"No. My door has a combination lock, and I didn't bother with my wallet. With an open bar, there was no need."

He held up her wrap and slipped it over her shoulders. Unable to resist, he traced one finger down the soft skin of her neck. His body responded with a leap of arousal. "I'm parked out back," he managed to squeeze out of his suddenly arid throat. He'd never look a gift horse in the mouth, but her offer was more than he'd expected, and a fantasy come true. She wasn't drinking, so it wasn't a drunken offer. She appeared serious and honest, but he gave her the chance to back out. "Are you sure?"

"Are you chickening out?" She took his hand and tugged him toward the back exit.

"I'm in, if you are."

She stopped and planted her hands on her hips. She raised her chin and stared right into his eyes. "Neil Buch, I'm not getting any younger. I made you an offer. I want a yes or no answer. One night. Nothing more."

He held back his frown that this was to be a one-night thing. "Yes, Julia Abrams, I am interested." He grasped her hand, and before his heart knew what was happening, he was opening the passenger door to his Lexus and helping her in. He closed the door and hurried around to his side, and by the time he got there, she was leaning back and smiling at him. No second thoughts there, at least none he could detect.

·❤· ❤· ❤·❤·❤·

Chapter Three

"Come inside." He opened the door and waited for her to enter. "Can I get you a drink?" He hung their jackets in the hall closet when he turned back, she was standing before him, her dress discarded on the floor. "Holy bit bucket." He groaned.

She was glorious. All curves and white lace, including her garter belt. She was a man's wet dream. He was definitely starting to like Berry Cove!

"Holy what?"

"Holy bit bucket," he repeated. "That's a euphemism for the place where discarded files go in a computer. "Kind of like saying holy cow, in awe."

She frowned for a moment, then winked. "Don't just stand there," she waggled her fingers. "You're wearing entirely too many clothes." She had his tie off and shirt unbuttoned before he could breathe. She grabbed him by the hand and led him down the hall to the master bedroom. Spinning around, she planted a breath-stealing, bone-melting kiss on his lips, then lay down on the bed and gestured him forward.

He kicked off his shoes and shed his pants. He paused, taking it all in.

"Are you coming?" she nibbled her lip nervously.

"I'm committing this to memory because things like this don't happen in real life. You are the most beautiful woman I've ever seen."

"No talking. Come on, Neil, I have needs." The faint pink in her cheeks showed she wasn't as confident as she pretended.

Her haste was as unnerving as it was arousing. He'd analyze it later. For now, he wanted her as much as she seemed to want him. "As you wish." He nibbled her sweet lips and fumbled with the pins in her hair. A long time later, he steered them both into heaven.

***

Something woke Neil from a deep sleep. He cocked his head to listen. Was someone in his house? Reality hit him like a jolt of electricity. Julia. He rolled over. She was gone!

"Seriously?" he grumbled and climbed out of bed. Grabbing a robe, he searched from room to room. She was gone. He glanced out the front window in time to see a taxi pull away.

"Crap." *What had he done wrong?* They'd been more than compatible and had made love twice, chatting and laughing between as they shared a bag of Cheezies in bed. He'd woken at five to find her curled up in his arms, snoring softly.

"You're not getting away that easily, Julia Abrams." He muttered and climbed into the shower. "We clicked. I know we did." He laughed. *Clicked?* They'd set his sheets on fire after a night of slow dancing. He was almost ready to declare that he loved her. He wouldn't have believed love at first sight was a thing, but now he had no doubt. He'd been attracted by her beauty and quickly fell for her upbeat personality and eager love for her community. She had a great sense of humor and was kind and compassionate. She certainly hadn't struck him as a one-and-done kind of girl.

·♥·♥·♥·♥·♥·

Chapter Four

J ulia paced up and down in the small crowd gathered for the Fall
Foliage Fly. She'd snuck home from Neil's and choked down
a light breakfast. All she had to do now was run the race without
bumping into him. She'd never had a one-night stand before and
had panicked. She couldn't bear to stick around and find out that it
was just a one-off...even if that was what she asked for. Better to do
the dumping than to be the one dumped.

She'd lived the nightmare of being dumped over and over. Never
again. She'd protect her heart at all costs, just the way she protected
her reputation. Thankfully, Neil didn't live here. He was just visiting
for two weeks. He'd be gone before she knew it. She pushed away the
ache the thought created. Their instant connection had felt special.

"Julia! What are you doing way back here?" Tamara, her blonde
friend, and neighbor asked. "You're always up front. Faster runners,
first."

"Yeah, I stayed up too late at the wedding. I'm not going to be
speedy today. Thought I'd hide out with you slow-pokes." Tamara
was a reluctant runner and had only joined to help out the cause.

With a one-hundred-dollar entry fee, plus optional pledges, it was a great way to contribute.

"I saw you dancing with that guy. You were still dancing when Jarod and I left. Who is he?"

"Neil. He's Maxim's friend from college. I was just being nice, hanging out with him, so he didn't feel alone. You know, doing the mayor thing."

"Mayor thing my tattered undies. You were totally into him. He must be a trooper to dance with you that long. How are his feet? He must be practically lame!"

Julia laughed. "Surprisingly, he taught me how to waltz. We even did the faster dances. He's a great lead. About halfway through the second song, I quit stomping him to death."

He *was* an incredible dancer. She'd felt so talented and loved in his arms. She pushed the thought away. "Are you ready for this?"

"Ready and unwilling. You still coming to dinner later?"

"You know it." She bent at the waist to stretch out her legs. They were unusually stiff this morning, and she knew why. She grinned, hoping Tamara didn't see it. An announcement came through the PA telling the runners it was time to line up, and before long, they were off and running. She'd successfully avoided running into Neil. Maybe he'd stayed home. A girl could hope.

The crowd of runners was all bunched up, and she rethought her plan to hide in the pack. Running full out would burn off some stress. Slowly, the pack thinned, and by the end of the first kilometer, she was hitting her stride without dodging too many people. Panting, Tamara kept pace beside her.

"Good morning, ladies."

She turned as Neil slowed his stride to run beside her. "I nearly missed the whole race. Guess I slept in." He cast a sly glance at her.

"Ya, slow dancing at weddings will do that to you," Tamara quipped between gasps.

Neil laughed. "Julia, can I buy you dinner tonight?"

"Thanks for the offer. I have to decline." She sucked in a few breaths as she ran, speeding her pace slightly. "I have plans. I'm going to dinner at Tamara's." She jabbed her thumb toward her friend.

"You should come too. Julia can pick you up," Tamara offered. "Dinner's at six. See you then." She dropped back, gasping.

"Later!" Neil called, a grin sliding over his face.

No way did she want to have dinner with Neil. Nope. She'd have to make an excuse. She pushed her pace, speeding up just slightly. He loped along beside her, barely breathing hard. One kilometer passed, then another. She pushed harder, trying to leave him behind.

"Trying to outrun me?" he asked without any signs of shortness of breath.

"Yes. No." She kept up her pace, though it was killing her to do so. Too much '*exercise*' and not enough sleep was taking its toll.

Neil didn't reply. He just jogged beside her. They crossed the finish line side by side, and she veered right, away from him.

Two minutes later, he was at her side. "I grabbed you a recovery tray." He held out a cardboard tray containing a handful of nuts, half a banana, and a glass of fruit juice.

"Thanks," she said, meaning it. She'd been prepared to skip the snack, just to avoid him, but was glad he'd thought of her.

"You're welcome."

She walked slowly up and down the parking lot of City Hall, where the run ended as she consumed the treats.

"You seem upset," he said at last, pacing alongside her. "Did I offend you last night? Did you not enjoy yourself?"

The genuine puzzlement in his voice hit her square in the guilt gene. "It was fine."

He winced. "Ouch."

"Okay," she ground out. "It was more than fine." She stopped walking and let him get close. "You were a stellar lover," she whispered. "I'm just not looking for long term."

"Okay. It surprises me, but I can respect that. Since I'm only here for a short time, can we have a short-term friendship?"

She scrunched up her face and scratched her head. Every molecule of her body wanted to scream yes. "Let me think about it. I'll pick you up for supper at ten to six." She tossed her empty tray in the compost bin and rushed to her car.

She sat behind the wheel, wondering what Tamara was thinking, inviting him to dinner. There was no way he'd back out, and she couldn't either. She was stuck with him, and it irritated her that she wasn't mad about it. She was looking forward to seeing the persistent man.

Chapter Five

"Here we are," Julia said as she slipped her car into first and shut off the engine. She yanked on the emergency brake with more force than was necessary.

"Nice house."

"It's cute." Tamara and Jarod lived in a small 1950s bungalow they'd refurbished to be more energy-efficient. It was adorable, but not much bigger than Julia's apartment. Eventually, she'd own a house, but she wasn't rushing into it. There was a charming house on Birch Bay that she'd love to have if it ever came up for sale.

Tamara greeted them with enthusiasm and invited them in. Childish screams erupted down the hallway. The house was clean, despite the toys and books littering every flat surface. "Dinner is in ten minutes. Jarod is in the kitchen. He'll make you a drink. I need to corral the hooligans."

"Hooligans?" Neil asked.

"Amy and Angie, four-year-old twins." Julia provided the information as Tamara rushed off.

"Let me get your coat," Neil said, setting down the gift bag he carried.

"Thanks." He hung up both coats, and she led him into the kitchen where Jarod was chatting with Maxim and Trudy, the happy couple from last night's wedding. Max and Trudy were delaying their honeymoon for a while.

She introduced Neil to Jarod, who owned Berry Cove's Honda dealership.

The men shook and stared at each other intently while still holding hands. Some sort of mystical man-thing passed between them, and they nodded solemnly.

Tamara returned to the kitchen, one daughter clinging to each hand. She made quick introductions. Neil squatted down to their level and offered his hand.

"Hi. I'm Neil. I'm new in town and looking for friends. Can you lovely ladies recommend anyone?" They both gaped at him like he was the craziest thing they'd ever seen, and like a balloon bursting, they started chatting so fast Julia could barely keep up.

In minutes, they led him to the table and insisted he sit between them. The man had a gift for kids. Dinner was a loud, entertaining event with a few spilled drinks and lots of laughter. They shared the wine Neil had brought and then another bottle.

"He's a keeper," Tamara whispered way too loudly as they headed to the door.

"Shush." Julia hissed. "He'll hear you."

"Well, he's a good guy. You could do worse. I can see why you danced so long. He's a hunk and so good with kids. You want kids, don't you?"

"If I ever find a man, which is doubtful, I would like kids. I love kids. Though I'm a bit upset that the girls cast me aside for a stranger." She laughed; her heart full to bursting.

"I'm totally shocked. They're usually shy of people they don't know."

"Thanks for a lovely evening," Neil said as they slid into their coats. "I really enjoyed myself."

"Come back anytime," Jarod said.

***

It was a week before he saw her again. He texted every morning and again every evening with offers of breakfast, lunch, or dinner. Once, he brazenly suggested hooking up. That one met with utter silence instead of a refusal. Lesson learned.

Friday, they went out to dinner at the local pizza joint. Dinner was relaxed and delicious. They lingered for hours chatting and getting to know each other. He held up Julia's coat so she could slip into it, and they stepped out into the falling snow.

"Oh, it's beautiful," she exclaimed. "It looks like heaven out here." The temperature had shot up five degrees while they were inside. It felt barely below freezing.

"Perfect for walking," Neil agreed.

"The park isn't far," she offered. "There are some lovely tree-lined paths."

"So says the mayor," he teased and offered his elbow. "Shall we?"

They turned left down a bike path, and in under a minute, they entered the park that ran behind Tamara's house. The park morphed into a greenspace that ran for several blocks past houses, condos, and three apartment complexes.

"I love walking here. I run here all summer," she said. "In winter, I stick to better paths. This one tends to ice over since they can't plow low enough to clear the ice without disturbing the gravel."

"It's pretty." He grasped her hand and held it in his.

They followed the red-shale path as it wandered through playground areas, between trees, and alongside grassy fields. The path was well-lit and easy walking. Gaily illuminated evergreens adorned their route. She was proud of how the town lit trees in every park. Christmas cheer was popping up everywhere, and it was barely the middle of October.

"This is my favorite spot." She paused to push the lightest dusting of snow off a slat bench before sitting down. "I love sitting here mornings and evenings, when it's quiet and peaceful."

He sad beside her and placed his arm behind her on the bench's back. They watched the snow fall for several minutes. "Have you thought about what I asked the other day?" he queried.

Her mind foundered to recall the question, which was crazy because it had plagued her for days. "I don't know." *Did she want to date him?*

"Come on. What have you got to lose? A few dates and then I'm out of here before Christmas. I'd really like to get to know you better."

"I suppose," she said after an uncomfortably long pause. *Before Christmas? Hadn't he been planning on two weeks? Christmas was nearly two full months away.*

"You don't sound certain. We'd be going in, knowing it's short-term. You wouldn't be caught unaware when it was over." His pause was equally long. "Can I ask why you're so wary?"

"You can ask." The joke fell flat. "Look, Neil. You seem like a nice guy. Polite, funny, good in bed. But I'm not looking to date. I've been down that road, and it always ends in heartache."

"I'm sorry that you've been hurt. Is there anyone I need to 'address' about it?"

She laughed wryly. "My mother. My grandmother. Jimmy Ripkin. Todd Wong?" Just saying their names hurt. Especially the first two. They'd hurt her the worst by showing her she was totally unlovable.

"I think this requires further discussion. I'd like to know more, if you don't mind sharing."

She jumped up, unwilling to talk about it. She started back toward her car. He followed beside her and slipped his arm under hers, so they were walking with interlinked arms. The simple contact settled something inside her heart. "Mom dumped me at my grandmother's when I was six." She choked on the last word.

"What? Who does that?" His voice was dark with anger.

"A woman bent on singing in Nashville. She abandoned me for her career. My grandmother believed her when she said it was just for a month. Fat lot she knew. One month became two. Two became a year. I watched out the front window every night, hoping she'd come home. For three years I waited, my heart crushed a little more every day, until it snapped in two."

"Oh my gosh. That's terrible. Nobody deserves that. You're worth so much more." He squeezed her hand.

"Or not. My grandmother resented me. She was...for lack of a better term, a serial dater. She was in her early sixties and ran around with every older, single man in town. And probably some of the married ones too. More than once, she told me I was killing her dating life. She was ecstatic when I turned twelve and she could leave me alone all night." Her heart squeezed at the memory, and tears rolled down her face.

She rebuilt the icy mental wall that was melting under his care. She couldn't go soft now. "The whole town knew. Everyone. Most took pity on me, but some seemed to think I was cut from the same cloth."

"Jeez."

She continued before he could say anything more. Now that she'd started, she wanted to get this all out, then he'd know why she didn't want to see him, and why she wasn't worthy of him. "Jimmy was certain that after a few dates, I'd put out. He dumped me after I gave him a black eye for insisting. Todd wasn't much better. He just dumped me for another woman. I'm undatable," she warned him. "I'm from a bad seed. You don't want to be around me."

"Screw that. You're a kind and generous woman who gives everything to this town. I do want to date you. Just because some people can't see your worth doesn't mean others don't. You were Trudy's maid of honor – that says something. Tamara and Jarod love you, so do their kids. Even without those people, I could see your worth. You are a valuable person in your own right. To hell with the idiots." He grabbed her shoulders and gave her a little shake.

"Easy for you to say."

"Damn right! Is there anything else you'd like to *confess*?" He put an ironic emphasis on the last word.

"Nope. Isn't that enough?" She pulled away and strode ahead to the car. She climbed in and started it before grabbing her snowbrush and getting back out.

"Stay inside," Neil said. "I'll brush it off for you."

Rather than helping relieve the burden she carried, her confession had chilled her through, so she gave him the brush and hopped in. It wasn't any warmer in the car, but she appreciated the gesture. Before the car was warm, Neil joined her.

"At the risk of pushing my limits, when can I see you again?" He faced her, his expression serious and hopeful.

A tiny crack appeared in the wall around her heart. "Next week?"

He fist pumped the air before clamping his seatbelt shut. "I'll take it."

She followed him into his house, thinking his enthusiasm was endearing. "I can't believe I'm here," she muttered under her breath.

"I heard that," he answered.

"Of course, you did," she grumbled.

"I heard that too." He turned to face her. "Relax, Julia. Low key. No pressure. Friendship and nothing more. I'm not even going to press for friends with benefits."

"I appreciate that." More than he'd ever know. She was in uncharted territory here. He had no idea how deeply he affected her equilibrium. She wanted to believe his eager attitude toward being with her was real, not a put-on, and not all about sex. But she'd been down that bumpy road before. She wasn't going to let her heart whisper sweet nothings until she let down her guard.

·❤·❤·❤·❤·❤·

Chapter Six

When Neil woke the next morning, she was gone. Again. "Dang woman." She'd come over willingly. She'd suggested staying after she had two glasses of wine. She hadn't been drunk, but she'd seduced him and vanished.

What was it about him, about them, that she couldn't face in the light of day? He thought he'd convinced her that he liked her, that he wanted to spend time with her. Where had he gone wrong?

He scraped his hands down his face. Coffee. He needed coffee to get his brain going. He hadn't slept right since he met Julia, and the lack of sleep left him too foggy to puzzle out her behavior. He stumbled to the kitchen and hit the start button on the coffee pot. Thank heaven for his ingrained habit of setting a new pot the minute he emptied the old one.

Mug in hand, he stood at the dining room's French doors and stared out at the enormous yard. Max could put a tennis court back there. In the distance, behind a thick row of trees, he could just make out the roof of Max and Trudy's house. He'd like nothing more than to tromp through the unmarred snow for a brain-clearing chat. Since they were leaving on their honeymoon, a chat was out of the question. Who else could he talk to? There had to be a way to figure out Julia. He pulled his phone from the pocket of his gray sweats. He'd traded numbers with Jarod. Would it be bad form to talk to him?

Probably.

· ♥ · ♥ · ♥ · ♥ · ♥ ·

The coffee shop was quiet. There wasn't a single soul inside except for Jarod, who sat at a table, his dark hair covered in a navy toque. "Morning," Max greeted Jarod. "Sorry for imposing."

"Morning. You said it's important."

"It is. Let me get you a coffee." They shared some casual conversation, and finally Jarod asked him why he had called.

"It's about Julia," Neil confessed after looking around to ensure nobody was within earshot. "I like her. A lot. She keeps putting up walls. Just when I think I've scaled them, or knocked a hole in them, she fortifies them by vanishing."

"Ouch." Jarod fiddled with his mug, poured in more creamer, and looked Neil dead in the eye. "Julia's had a hard life. She's been friends with Tamara since they were kids. I can't give you details; that's for her to share."

"She told me about being abandoned by her family."

"Then you know it led to self-esteem issues, right? She doesn't feel worthy of anyone's love. I mean, Julia's never said anything, I sure wouldn't have sussed it out, but Tamara worries about her and has mentioned it."

"Self-esteem issues?" He considered it. It didn't make any sense to him. Julia was pretty, funny, smart, and she was the freaking mayor. How could she not believe in her own worth? "She's so great," he said after too long a pause.

"You know it. I know it. Everyone in town knows it. Except Julia. If you want to break through those walls, you have to convince her she's worthy of more than a one-night stand."

Heat crept up Neil's face. "How did you know?" He buried his face in his hands and scrubbed his fingers through his hair.

"She confessed to Tamara. And you didn't hear that from me. I'd never break a confidence, but you have a reputation in the gaming world as an upright guy. Good to your employees, generous with charity. If I didn't know all about you, I'd tell you to go straight to hell."

"Um, thanks?" He drummed his fingers on the table. "How did you know who I am?"

"Your name, for one. Plus, I know that Maxim has a friend in the gaming industry. He mentioned you once. *Crisis Eleven* was the hottest first-person shooter game in a decade. The jokes and puns took gaming to a whole new level. Word on the street is that it got you a billion-dollar buyout deal. Have you told Julia?"

"No. I expect she thinks I'm a bum. She seems overly concerned that I find a job." He chuckled.

"Look, man, if Julia thinks you're a bum and still shows up, it means she likes you. A lot. Stay strong, bro. And your money won't impress her, but your character might."

"Thanks. I'll keep that in mind. She'll never know I talked to you."

"Unless Tamara tells her I met with you."

"I'll debug that code when or if it glitches."

Okay, self-esteem issues he could deal with. He'd never had them himself, but he sure knew others who did. His former assistant had been the shyest, least-confident woman he'd ever met. After a few years of working with him and being built up, she was outgoing and could tackle anything. Demanding a raise proved that she now knew her worth.

On his way home, he stopped at Betty's Blooms and ordered a winter greens bouquet. "Can you deliver that to Mayor Abram's office?"

"Absolutely. Did you want to put in a card?" The shopkeeper gestured to a rack of pretty note cards.

"Yes, please." He scrawled a message and signed his name before sealing it shut and handing it over. *Let Operation Build Up begin*!

·❤·❤·❤·❤·❤·

Chapter Seven

Alight knock sounded on Julia's partially closed office door on Tuesday morning. "Come in," she called. Luckily, she wasn't too deep into her work yet. She was just about to review next year's proposed budget. Berry Cove's fiscal year started in March, the month the town was incorporated. She glanced up to see her temporary receptionist.

"What's up, James?"

The twenty-something youth stepped inside and thrust a floral package forward. "This was just delivered for you. He set it gently on her desk, ensuring it didn't tip.

She stared warily at the package. Obviously, someone had sent her flowers. "Does it say who it's from?" She eyed it warily. *Was this a joke?*

"No, ma'am. The delivery guy said there was a card inside. I tipped him from the envelope in Trudy's, er, my, desk."

"That's what it's there for. Thanks, James." She nodded, and he left the room, though she could read the reluctance to go in his slow steps.

She waited until he was out of sight before standing and glaring at the package. Finally, she decided she might as well open it. She slit the tape closing the tall package shut with her silver letter opener, and slowly peeled back the paper. She drew in an awed breath. Floral freshness washed over her. It smelled like Christmas. Red and white roses nestled amid spruce, pine, and cedar. She lifted the crystal vase from the paper and set it on her desk.

She dropped into her chair and stared. It was lovely, but who would send such a thing? Fingers trembling, she reached for the card. She turned the dark green envelope over and over in her hand before lifting the flap. Precise masculine box letters filled the card.

JULIA

THESE FLOWERS ARE LOVELY, BUT THEY CAN'T HOLD A CANDLE TO YOUR BEAUTY AND INNER GLOW.

ALWAYS,

NEIL

The card dropped from her suddenly numb fingers. She straightened it on her desk, precisely aligning it with the edge and holding the four corners with her index fingers and thumbs. *Always? What did that mean? Who sent a card like that to someone they barely knew?*

After several long moments of contemplation, she decided not to fret over it and just enjoy the flowers. She recycled the paper, made sure the vase had adequate water, and sat staring at the lovely arrangement. She should call and thank him, but after sneaking out again the other night, the thought of speaking to him had her suddenly nervous and more than a little wary.

Eventually, she got back to work, but her mind and eyes kept straying to the flowers. James knocked again.

"Another package." He slid the long flat box onto the table. "It's starting to feel like Christmas in here. Should I put up the tree?"

"I think not," she answered. "Never before December first."

With a nod, he slipped from the room.

She eyed the package warily, somehow knowing it came from Neil. He was up to something. What was he trying to achieve?

She pushed the box to the side and went back to work. Eventually, curiosity got the better of her.

Inside the plain brown wrapper was the familiar navy and silver wrapping of a *Guilty Pleasures* box. She almost drooled in anticipation of the heavenly chocolate delights from a local chocolatier. She opened the navy envelope taped to the inner wrap. This time, Neil's manly script referred to her sweet personality. Heat rose in her face as she slid the unopened box into her desk. Whatever he was up to wasn't going to work. No way. No how.

Wednesday and Thursday brought a wine basket, a fruit basket, and a hand-knit mitten and scarf set. She should have texted him to thank him, but she feared opening herself to being hurt. She'd slept with him. Twice. She'd agreed to see him again. This felt like more. Like he was trying to woo her. The idea was ridiculous. He wanted the same thing she did, a couple of quick rolls in the sheets. Didn't he? And if he was unemployed, how was he affording these luxurious gifts?

Friday at ten, she groaned when James knocked on her door. "What is it this time, James?" she grumbled. She was fast losing her heart to Neil and didn't like the feeling.

"It's a dinner and dancing invitation," Neil said.

Her head jerked up so fast her neck cracked. She massaged it with her left hand. "Dang." She sighed. No avoiding him now. "Neil."

"Oh, so you are speaking to me. I thought maybe you were an NPC."

"A what?" Her voice cracked in confusion.

"Non-playable character."

"Sure?" His explanation did nothing to clear up her confusion.

"In video games," he elaborated. "NPCs are those characters that are part of the game, and no matter how you try and interact with them, you get the same canned response or no response at all." His voice lilted at the end, asking if she understood.

"Sorry, I don't game."

He clutched his chest like he was having a heart attack. "Tell me that's not true." He shook his head sadly. "We'll have to remedy that." He paused. "Will you go to dinner with me? Maybe dancing at the Road House later? And don't say you can't dance. I've proven that a fallacy already."

"No, thank you." She wanted to go so badly. His persistence over the week was wearing her down.

"Tomorrow night?" He ran down the days of the next week, and she refused every offer. "Is it me?" he asked, seeming half serious.

"It's me. We had this discussion. I'm not interested in a relationship. Friendship, maybe."

"No." His pause was deliberate. "You're scared."

She jerked to her feet. "So what if I am? There isn't a life rule book that says I have to date, or marry, or have kids."

Her heart trembled when he reared back at her vehemence. His eyes darkened in hurt. His shoulders hunched and then slowly straightened.

"Okay. I'll go. Goodbye, Julia." He walked slowly from the office, closing the door soundlessly behind him.

She'd have preferred him slamming it in anger.

·❤·❤·❤·❤·❤·

Chapter Eight

Neil spent the next four days trying to figure out what he was going to do. At first, he attributed his hurt to simple rejection. He'd already realized that he liked Julia. A lot. Everywhere he went, she was there.

He saw her at the skating rink, at the winter carnival, and at the grocery store. He was in the real estate office when she walked by. He almost ran after her. Instead, he started looking at houses as he'd intended when he entered the office. He'd buy one and have his belongings moved in. He was here to stay, because like it or not, he was totally smitten. With her, and with Berry Cove.

Love at first sight came to mind. A ridiculous concept at best. Still, catching rare glimpses of her was better than never seeing Julia again. He was an idiot. A besotted idiot. He trudged up Maxim's walk to drop off his key to the guest house.

"Come in," Trudy exclaimed, swinging the door wide. "Maxim's not here. Do you want some coffee?"

"I'd take a shot of whiskey."

"Oh no, what's wrong?" She grabbed him by the arm and dragged him into the kitchen without even letting him take off his shoes.

"Sit." She shoved him into an oak chair and bustled around pouring coffee. She slopped some Bailey's in both mugs and pushed his toward him. "Talk to me."

They didn't know each other well; they'd only met a couple of times before the wedding. Maxim married her and loved her, and that went a long way - it meant Neil could trust her as well. Besides, she was Julia's friend, which could only help, couldn't it?

"What is wrong with your boss?"

"With Julia?" She laughed. "Since I got back from the honeymoon, she's bitchy. I think she's in love. She doesn't eat. She's not sleeping. She's grumpier than a grizzly in the spring. Why do you ask?"

"I keep trying to ask her out. She refuses."

"O-oh." Trudy's eyes went wide, and her mouth formed an O. "I didn't know it was you." She giggled. "You're going to have to chase her down."

"I thought men were supposed to back away when a woman said no?" Now he was totally confused.

"Generally, yes. Not this time. Now that I know it's you, I say go for it. Julia's been alone too long." Trudy looked solemn. "Her entire life. Keep after her. She just needs to know that you're in it for the long haul."

***

Julia glared at Trudy as she danced down the street on their way to the town square's tree lighting ceremony. Max was meeting them there.

"This is going to be so much fun!" Trudy declared.

"Berry Cove needs a new tradition," Julia said. "We should run a contest, so I don't have to do this. Let's pick a random kid from the crowd to hit the switch."

"Don't be silly. Traditions are important, and the mayor has always lit the tree."

"I could call in sick."

Trudy stopped, hands on her hips, and glared. "Julia, you might be my boss, but you're also my best friend, and I've had enough of this—of this crap. You've been unbearable since the wedding. Grow up. Either suck it up and move on with your life, or ask the danged man out."

"What man?"

Trudy rolled her eyes so hard Julia thought they might get stuck. "Um, Neil," she said in a Valley Girl voice. "He's as miserable as you are. Frankly, you're both driving Max and me nuts with the pouting and whining."

"I didn't know he was still in town."

Another eye roll. "He bought that house on Birch Bay that you like. He was looking at listings with a realtor when the owners came in to list it. He snapped it up right away."

"What? I've been waiting for it to go on the market."

Trudy looked guilty.

"What did you do?" Julia snapped, her short temper reaching its limit.

"I might have mentioned it." Trudy winced. "I didn't mean to. We were talking when he came to dinner. It sort of slipped out."

Tears threatened. It felt like the world was ganging up on her.

"Forgive me?" Trudy begged, her hands clenched, prayerlike, in front of her heart.

"I shouldn't. But fine. You're forgiven." She tried her best to smile. "Anything else I need to know about? Any other ways you sabotaged my life?"

"Nope. Cross my heart." Trudy made the motion.

She had a guilty look on her face, but Julia didn't push the issue. One more thing would steal the last of her resolve, and she'd bolt on the tree lighting. The only thing keeping her here was knowing there was an election next year, and she didn't want to screw up her chances by annoying the diehard Christmas lovers in town, and, admittedly, miss out on her favorite time of year.

The low sounds of carolers reached her as they drew near the park. This *was* her favorite time of year. She loved the holidays, and she adored how the local chorale group dressed in period costumes and strolled around town singing everything from traditional religious

songs to secular classics and modern hits. A local pastor, Irwin My-
ers, did a version of *Hallelujah* that would make angels weep.

Vendors lined the park selling everything from hot roasted al-
monds and hazelnuts to cocoa to chocolates. There was a food truck
selling deep-fried pickles, and another selling bacon maple lattes. It
was a food lover's paradise. The air was heavy with the tasty aromas
of chocolate, cider, and fried food.

A fabulous Santa in a very realistic suit sat on his chair with a line
of excited children snaking toward him. He ho ho hoed happily, a
genuine smile on his face. He flashed a wink in her direction.

Though she didn't want to cheer up, she'd rather wallow in
self-pity, a smile blossomed in her heart for the joy in the moment,
and she found herself joining in when the carolers stopped in front
of her to sing *We Wish You a Merry Christmas*.

They paused at the end, accepted the applause, and strolled off,
revealing that Maxim and Neil had been standing behind them.

Her heart plummeted and soared. Neil looked incredible in his
heavy red, black, and white buffalo wool sweater and matching cap.

Max scooped Trudy into his arms and kissed her long and deep.
Julia turned away. She glanced back to see Neil with an equally
uncomfortable look on his face. He quirked an eyebrow as if to say,
"What can you do?" A laugh bubbled out of her.

"Can I buy you a beverage?" he asked, stepping forward to stand
just outside of her personal bubble.

"I can't."

His face fell.

"At least not until after I light the tree. If you don't mind waiting." She hadn't planned on saying yes. The response just popped
out after he sounded so eager and unsure. His smile rivalled the
brightest Christmas tree.

"I'll wait," he declared.

And he did. He walked alongside her to the portable stage near
the tree and stood at the side while she gave her short speech and hit
the switch.

He whistled and clapped when the lights came on as if she'd done something miraculous. He waited patiently for forty-five minutes as she spoke with her constituents and made a few notes on her phone about their concerns. Finally, she was free.

"Whew! I'm done. I'll take that drink now." She smiled.

"Here, or can I take you inside someplace warm? I hear the pub has a hot drink special all week. We could get a bite to eat." He stuffed his hands in his pockets.

"I'd like that."

"You would?" he asked incredulously.

"I would." She meant the words. How could she not? This man had waited six weeks for her. She hadn't expected him to stick around past the first week. Especially after she repeatedly refused to be seen with him or accept his calls.

He made a broad *after you* gesture and trailed after her from the park. He didn't complain when she was stopped again and again by people she knew. He stood quietly behind her until her conversations were done. Finally, they stepped into the warmth of the pub.

"Sorry for all the delays," she said, hanging her jacket on a hook on the end of the tall bench seat of their table.

"You're a busy woman. I didn't mind waiting for you."

She wondered if he meant more than just today. Had he minded her ignoring him for weeks, hoping he'd go away? She blushed. "Sorry for being stubborn."

He looked thoughtful. Their server arrived and they ordered Hot Rum Toddies. After she walked away, he said, "Julia, I like you. A lot. I think about you every day. I was struck senseless the moment I saw you, and every minute we spent together, I grew to like you more. You're worth waiting for." His voice rang with a sincerity that left her breathless. She knotted her fingers together on the table.

"Um. Thanks?" She didn't know what to say. After their few dates, all the gifts, and his persistence, she almost believed him.

He smiled warmly. "I'm not asking for forever. I'm asking to see you again. One date at a time. I'd like to take a relationship with you one day at a time and see where it goes. Maybe the heat between us fizzles out, maybe it grows. I'm okay with either. I just want to see more of you." He inhaled loudly and swallowed. "If you want platonic, I'm okay with that too."

A giggle burst from her throat. "Indeed?" She gave him her best *I don't believe you* look.

"Okay, I'll do my best to be patient." He grasped her hands in his and gently separated her fingers and massaged each one. "Julia Abrams, I've waited my whole life for a woman like you. No, I haven't been waiting for just anyone; I've been waiting for you. Julia, will you go out with me?"

How could she possibly resist?

They were compatible in interests. They shared the same sense of humor and sense of charity. They were definitely fiery in bed. Delicious fire. She liked everything about him, especially his persistence in pursuing her.

"One week," he said, before she could answer. "Just give me a week."

"I'll tell you what," she said, her expression deadpan. "I'll give you two weeks." She'd take this slowly, as slow as he'd let her, but there was no denying that Neil was everything she wanted in a lifetime partner. She just needed to be certain he wasn't going to damage her heart. She'd never survive another heartbreak.

·♥·♥·♥·♥·♥·

Chapter Nine

The next two weeks were glorious. They went to Christmas concerts and plays. They tobogganed and went for snowmobile rides. They shopped for furniture and accessories for Neil's new home. Neil sat in her office and puttered on his laptop, working out details for his new business venture, while she worked on her paperwork.

She was stunned to learn how much he'd sold his gaming company for.

He had great promotional ideas for the upcoming election, ones that would catapult her to the top without maligning her opponents.

On Christmas Eve, they went to Trudy and Max's for a quiet dinner. The house was redolent with the smell of roast beef and gravy. Puffy and delicious Yorkshire puddings made the perfect complement to the tender beef and roasted potatoes. Stuffed to the limit, they carried their wine into the cozy family room.

Max stoked the fire. "I love this room," Julia declared. "The fireplace is exquisite." She stroked the hand-carved mantle and smoothed her fingers over the stone before moving to nestle against Neil's side on the sofa.

"It's cozy," he agreed. "Look, I know it isn't Christmas Day yet, and it's early to give gifts, but I can't wait." He dug into his pants pocket and pulled out a deep purple box.

For a fraction of a moment, Julia's heart soared, and then she panicked until she realized the box was too big to be a ring box. She did a mental double-take. Did she want a ring? Yes! But not yet. It was too soon.

"Julia," Neil said. "I adore you. I love you." He flipped open the box to reveal a shining gold heart and diamond pendant. "It's too early to propose...but I'd like to propose that we turn this relationship more serious. I'd like to propose getting engaged to be engaged."

"What?" Her mind stumbled on his words. She shook her head to clear her thoughts.

"I want you to know that I'm ready to be engaged whenever you are. I'm suggesting we consider this relationship exclusive and acknowledge that we'll be engaged. Soon."

Max chortled. From the corner of her eyes, Julia saw Trudy elbow Max in the ribs.

"Engaged to be engaged," Julia repeated. It was the most ridiculous thing she'd ever heard. She loved it. She nibbled her lip in indecision.

Warmth and love washed over her along with an undeniable certainty that Neil was in this relationship for the long haul. He wasn't going to abandon her. He loved her the way she loved him. Heat and comfort soared through her. She loved Neil!

"Yes, Neil. I accept your proposal to be engaged to be engaged." She flung her arms around his neck and drew him close for a kiss. Her heart thundered in her ears, making them ring. Then, it settled into a calm, secure rhythm. "I love you, Neil Buch."

He cupped her face in his hands. "I love you, Julia Abrams. For now, and for always." Their lips met in a soft, caring caress filled with promise and hope for the future.

· ♥ · ♥ · ♥ · ♥ · ♥ ·

One More Time

Chapter One

Dara rested her hand on her baby bump and stared at her boss, Mayor Julia Abrams. She was way too tired and pregnant for this type of stress. "Really?" She shook her head. *No way on earth did she want to play host to Axel Justice.* "You can't be serious." Her stomach cramped. *She did not need that brand of stress.*

"Dead serious. Berry Cove needs you. I need you."

"I'm not a social person. I'm an accountant, for Pete's sake. Plus, I thought we were friends. How can you ask me to work with him?" She swallowed hard. "I can't. Fire me if you have to. But I can't."

"Why in the world not? Do you know him?" Julia frowned and smoothed her thick red hair. She tapped her fingers on her wooden desk. "Close the door, please."

This is it. This is where I get fired by one of my closest friends. Dara closed the door and sat in the chair across from Julia. "We've been friends since high school. You know I'd do anything for you."

"Except this?" Julia looked puzzled. "What's the big deal, Dara? Ninety percent of women would jump at the chance to rub shoulders with Axel Justice. He's only the biggest thing in hockey. Ever. Do you know how many trophies the man has won?"

"Literally at least one every year since he was drafted ten years ago. He holds more awards than any other player except Gretzky." *Lord, how she wished she didn't know.* It was too easy to remember everything about him, especially those deep brown eyes and his short dark hair. She refused to think about his five o'clock shadow against her skin. He'd been stuck in her dreams for eight and a half months.

"And he's gorgeous and single. Very single. He's considering running a major hockey school here. In Berry Cove. A permanent one. Year after year. We need this."

"I know we do. Just go ahead and fire me." She rested both hands on top of her baby bump. Knowing she had a child growing inside her was comforting somehow, despite the upcoming stresses of being a single mother. This time, her baby didn't calm Dara's jangling nerves.

Julia looked at her. Hard. She squinted. "Holy Christmas candles. Is he...?" she trailed off in disbelief.

Tears ran down Dara's cheeks. She nodded. "He is," she whispered, barely able to get the words past the Christmas-ball-sized lump lodged in her throat. "And he doesn't know about my baby. I don't want him to know."

"I'm going to need an explanation." Julia's voice was soft and sympathetic.

"Remember when I won that weekend at West Edmonton Mall? I went. I had a blast. My college roomie and I hit a bar. His team was there celebrating that night's massive win. We danced. We had a drink or two. Not enough to get careless. Just enough to cut loose. One thing led to another. We used protection, I'm not stupid." She sighed for what felt like the thousandth time since this conversation started. "Apparently, it didn't work." She shrugged.

"And you never told him?"

"No. He's a big star. He's always surrounded by women. I don't want that kind of life for my child. Look at me. I'm a simple, small-town girl. He's a superstar. Totally incompatible."

"Well, not totally, apparently," Julia smirked. "I'll let you off this time. But if this deal goes through, he'll be in town regularly, and you'll have to deal with him anyway. Are you sure you don't want to tell him now and get it over with? Rip off the bandage?"

"I need time to work up to this." Her chest hurt. "I really am sorry."

"I'll get James to do it. He's a great assistant. He's no athlete, but he is a hockey buff. He'll try hard. I do wish Trudy hadn't left us to work with Max."

"I'm not an athlete either."

"No, but you are a beautiful woman. I'm not above using that quality to get what will benefit our town, and in turn, us."

"Ah, pretty privilege, where you get more because you look good," she snarked, using air quotes. It wasn't like Julia to play underhanded. Something had to be going on. "What's the real deal?"

"Truth?" She fiddled with the tiny Grinch tree, with the bent top and enormous red Christmas ball, which sat on the corner of her desk. "The rink is bleeding money. Its expenses are triple its income. If we don't find a way to increase revenue, we either have to close it or eliminate all the free programs. Programs like free public skating, free teen shinny hockey, and seniors' figure skating. Either way, the whole town loses. I don't want to do that."

"I had no idea." She stared out the office window at the snow falling gently, trying to resolve the dilemma of being needed and terrified of the truth coming out.

"It costs a fortune to run the ice plant, and we've had to replace the Zamboni."

Dara stared down at her lap as she struggled to make a decision. The analog clock on the wall above the door loudly ticked away the seconds and added pressure. She loved this town, and Julia was one of her closest friends. She couldn't abandon them in their time of need. *Crap.* "I'll do it. I'll figure out a lie if I have to." Gosh, she hated trading on her looks. But Berry Cove was her home, and those programs were invaluable.

"Are you sure?" Compassion rang in her boss's voice.

"No." She laughed wryly. "But I'll do it."

"Excellent. I appreciate this more than you know." She reached into her drawer, pulled out a credit card, and slid it across the desk. "He'll be at Bean Brewed in fifteen minutes. Take him to the arena and all the other facilities he might need. Give him the grand tour. Take him to dinner. The works. Take him to see our fabulous Santa. Show him our Christmas spirit, so he can see how Berry Cove does up holidays. Don't forget to talk about all our other summer programs and festivals. We want this deal."

Dara stood and saluted. "Yes, boss. I'll do my best, boss." This was going to be the worst day of her life.

·❤·❤·❤·❤·❤·

Chapter Two

B erry Cove was the most enchanting town Axel had ever visited. The Christmas decorations were fabulous. Tons of lights. Santas, Grinches, trees. Sleighs and reindeer. Main Street looked like the North Pole. It made him nostalgic for the holidays he'd had with his family before he'd been chosen in the first round of the NHL draft all those years ago.

The people were friendly, but not pushy. He'd been in town for an hour and had signed a couple dozen autographs. Everyone had been polite when asking. In the past, he'd been pushed to his breaking point more than once by rabid fans, but not here. The manners shown today were refreshing. Crowd pressure was the major reason why he was leaving hockey. Of course, he was the only person who knew that. His manager was going to have a hissy fit when he found out.

He paused when he reached his destination.

Bean Brewed. What a clever name for a coffee shop.

He pushed the door open and stepped inside. The delicious scents of cocoa and heavenly coffee tickled his nose. Decorated in browns and creams, the shop was hopping. People ambled in, chatted, got drinks and baked goods, and ambled out again. The pace here was slower. He checked his watch. Someone from the mayor's office should arrive in about fifteen minutes. He grabbed a green tea and took a seat at a table with a clear view of the door to people-watch while he waited.

It wasn't long before the door swung open and a frigid breeze swept across him. He should have chosen a table further from the door. A beautiful brunette in a loose, knee-length, navy wool coat and a red and white striped scarf came in and stomped the snow off her boots.

His heart pounded. For a moment, he refused to believe his eyes. It was her. How many times had he thought he'd seen her and been wrong? This time, there was no doubt.

She lifted her head and scanned the room. Her gaze froze on him, and all the color drained from her face. Her eyes closed, and she frowned. She wiped her boots and strode toward him.

"Axel? I'm Dara Sanford. Nice to meet you." She offered her hand.

He stood and took it. Electricity jolted up his arm. *He'd found her!* There was only ever one person who had given him a shock like that. Until now, he thought he'd never see her again. His breath caught, and he held her hand for a moment too long. Reluctantly, he released her.

"Hi. Again," he said.

"I'm sorry? Have we met?" She set her tiny navy, bling-covered purse on the table and slid into the wooden chair opposite him. "I'm from the mayor's office."

He tilted his head and studied her. Oh, yeah. Definitely the woman who had made his evening fun, and his night the most passionate he'd ever spent. No other woman compared to her. She'd ruined his dating life.

They'd laughed and talked and danced. He'd have sworn they connected on a deeper level. "West Edmonton Mall in the hotel bar? Does that ring a bell? I'm glad I found you. You slipped away without giving me your number. But I could swear you said your name was Laurel."

Her sigh was like a punch to the solar plexes.

"Middle name. Can we just pretend that night didn't happen?" Her eyes pleaded with him.

"Dara, there is nothing that will make me forget the best night of my life."

"Um. Thanks?" Her wince was adorable. "Would you like a coffee or something? Maybe some of Mable's cherry-apple pie?" She seemed desperate to change the subject.

"Pie sounds good, and another green tea. What would you like? It's on me."

"It's on The Town of Berry Cove, but thank you. I'll just pop over and get it." She got up without taking her coat off and hurried to the counter. He sat down and watched her smiling interaction with the barista. She was lovelier than he remembered. After a brief moment, she came back empty-handed.

He raised an eyebrow in question.

"They're bringing it over."

The middle-aged woman behind the counter carried over a tray with his tea and pie, a drink topped with a mountain of whipped cream, and a cinnamon bun. "Couldn't have you lugging this heavy tray, Dara." She slid the tray onto the table. "Here you two go. Enjoy."

She smiled broadly at his thanks and hurried back to the counter, where another customer waited.

Dara unbuttoned her coat but didn't remove it. She had to be sweating because it was warm in here, even with the occasional icy breeze sweeping through.

"If you're cold, we could move to that table by the fireplace."

"No. I'm fine." She cut off a bite of cinnamon bun and got icing on her coat. "Dang."

"Maybe you should take your coat off."

"I guess." She slipped out of the coat and let it fall back over her chair. She picked up her mug and cradled it between her hands. She stared down into it like it held the secret of the universe.

She was hiding her face from him!

Why?

Were her cheeks pink?

"Is everything okay?" She seemed upset and not at all like the carefree woman he remembered.

"It's fine. Let me tell you about Berry Cove." She launched into a public relations expert's rundown on the town's festivals and attractions. They talked between bites. About the time she finished the sumptuous-looking roll, he was savoring the last bite of his delicious pie. "I think you'll be impressed with our arena," she said and finally gave him a friendly half-smile.

Maybe she was warming up to him. "I'm sure it will. I checked it out online."

"Why don't we head out and look it over. Then I'll answer any questions you have."

"That sounds good." He stood.

She rose to her feet, and for a second, her loose top pulled tight over her abdomen. That was definitely a baby bump. "Congratulations." He nodded toward the bump with a smile, though his heart dropped to his toes.

"Um. Thanks."

"What are you and your husband hoping for?" *Had he slept with a married woman? She wasn't wearing a ring, not now, not then. Was that why she gave a false name? He couldn't abide cheaters. Marriage was sacred.*

"No husband. Single mom." Her cheeks pinkened.

"Let me help with your coat." Relief flooded through him, and his heart gave a happy thump, then stalled for a second. She wasn't available. She was carrying another man's child and that put her firmly in the "not available" category.

She handed him her coat, and he held it open for her to slip her arms in. "Thank you."

She really seemed pleased by the simple gesture. As a kid, he'd been annoyed by his grandfather's insistence on old-world manners. Now, women seemed to appreciate them, and he wished the small courtesies were more common. People should take care of each other.

"My car or yours?"

Her question flashed a memory into his head. Him, asking her up to his room. 'My room or yours.' He'd never had a one-night stand, he had a firm rule against them because too many women would try and take advantage of his near-celebrity status. He hadn't known why he asked beyond the idea that he didn't want to leave her side, and the bar was closing. The heat that followed had burned into his brain like a brand.

"Why don't you drive?" he suggested. "That way I can look around and get to know the landmarks as you tell me about them."

"Murray Ratcliff, the caretaker, is waiting for us at the arena. We have two ice sheets, a small gymnasium for sports, two squash courts, a workout room with thirty machines, and a food court that is open during events. On the second floor, overlooking both arenas, is a private venue which includes a bar. The town of Berry Cove leases them the space."

"Sounds like heaven." They climbed into her no-nonsense Toyota and pulled out of the lot.

Dara focused on the road and still managed to point out the firehall, the town office, several thriving businesses, and the movie theater. The entire downtown core was lit with colored lights. Candy canes hung from the lamp posts, and store windows were filled with colorful holiday displays.

They paused at a light beside a group of carolers on a downtown corner. Their Victorian costumes were period perfect, if the movies he watched were accurate. One grey-haired, grey-bearded man in a top hat reminded Axel of Santa. Axel waved, and the old man grinned and waved back. He seemed a jolly sort.

They traveled through an older but well-maintained residential area, which was fully decorated with lights and holiday figures, and past the curling rink with its colorful tree. The town radiated Christmas. Looking at the lights, then at her very pregnant belly, he felt like Scrooge. Knowing she carried another man's baby stole his joy.

"Here we are." She turned into an enormous parking lot in front of a large cinderblock building. Three towering pines out front were festooned with bright, colorful lights, and there was an enormous Season's Greetings banner draped on one side of the building.

"It's bigger than I expected."

She parked and turned to look at him. "Didn't you investigate before you approached the mayor's office?"

"A college chum highly recommended the facility, and I checked it out online. The internet didn't do it justice. It's not the only one I'm investigating, but it shows promise. Shall we go in?"

"Sure." She struggled out from behind the wheel and took a moment to gain her footing before locking the car. "This is the main arena entrance. To the left is the fieldhouse entrance. Through it, you reach the gym, the running track I forgot to mention, and the other sports facilities. Of course, they are connected, making it easy to travel between the sides."

She minced her way toward the door. The falling snow had dusted the sidewalk. Someone needed to get out the shovel before a customer fell and was injured.

"Let me help you. It looks slippery ahead." The sidewalk shone with ice, and he wanted to touch her again, even if it was through her coat.

"Thanks." She placed her hand in the crook of his elbow.

A fortyish man came out carrying a bucket and began spreading deicer on the walkway. "Morning, Murray," she called out a cheerful greeting.

"Morning, Dara. Give me five minutes to finish here. I'll meet you inside."

Axel should have been focused on what was in the building, but he couldn't take his eyes off Dara. Even in the LED lighting, she was beautiful. Her hair glimmered, and her skin glowed. She looked healthy, but tired.

Was the baby keeping her awake at night?

Not your business, Axel.

"Over here is the food court." She led him to a cluster of six tables and chairs. To the side was a shelf of books festooned with garland. "That's our little free library. It's funny how often people come here without a way to occupy themselves while waiting. We also have this basket of fruit. When the town first put it out, intending to help some of our less fortunate citizens, someone kept taking all of it. Now, people take a piece and eat it. Some even leave a cash donation. Funny thing is, sometimes, it refills itself. Murray swears he isn't doing it and won't tell us who is."

"That's sweet." Not as sweet as she was. There was also an overflowing box of food for the food bank, and a bin of unwrapped toys labeled for the Santa Drive. Berry Cove must be a giving town. He hadn't considered local generosity before coming here, but it definitely a quality he admired, and a point in Berry Cove's favor.

"Let's sit and wait for our guide." He led her to a table. She shouldn't be on her feet. She was enormous. Judging by his older sister, she was due any time now. He sat opposite the chair she chose so he could see her lovely face.

"When are you due?"

"Not soon enough." She perched on the edge of a chair with a heartfelt sigh.

"You sound like my sister. For her last month, she hated her husband." He chuckled.

Something stirred in the back of his mind. A thought that he couldn't quite grasp. He ignored it. "What are your plans for when the baby comes?"

·♥· ·♥· ·♥· ·♥· ·♥·

Chapter Three

Sweet heaven. He looked good. Too good. Dara's heart tripped, and her overly emotional self sighed with happiness at seeing him again. She'd missed him.

But boy, he was nosy. "I've got a nice nest egg, and I'll get maternity benefits. When those run out, I'll return to work. My friend Jacinda runs Little Britches Daycare. She's saving me a spot." *Why in the world are you telling him your life story? Shut up before you reveal something better kept secret.*

"Won't it be difficult to raise a child alone?"

"Maybe." She shrugged. *Where in the heck was Murray?*

"Is the father chipping in?"

"Excuse me? How is that your business?" It was totally his business, not that she'd admit it. She struggled to her feet, getting up grew more difficult by the day. She paced the area, straightening chairs, and avoiding his gaze.

"It isn't my business. But judging by your reaction, and the fact that you haven't mentioned him, I'm guessing he's not in the picture." He paused. "I'd be pissed if someone had my child without telling me."

"Well, this baby isn't yours, so mind your own business."

Cheese on toast. She didn't mean to say that! Hopefully, he'd miss the slip and not connect the very obvious dots.

He jumped to his feet. "Jeez. I hadn't even considered that." He squinted at her like he was trying to figure something out.

"When, exactly, are you due, Dara?" he demanded softly.

Busted!

"Soon."

He pulled out his phone and fiddled with the screen. He looked up at her and shoved the phone into his jacket pocket. "The internet gestation calculator suggests that this child could be mine." His cold stare terrified her. "Is this my baby?"

Gray spots danced in front of her eyes. Everything went dim. *Shoot, she was fainting.*

·❤·❤·❤·❤·❤·

"Dara? Dara? Are you with me?"

Slowly, reality returned. She opened her eyes. Axel's anxious face hovered over her. Beyond him, the ceiling spun. She closed her eyes again.

"You fainted. I barely caught you. We need to get you to a doctor. This could be serious."

"Should I call an ambulance?" Murray asked.

Now, he shows up.

"No!" She opened her eyes again. "I must be dehydrated. I'll be fine. Can I have a drink?" Murray scuttled away and came back with a bottle of water.

"Let's sit you up," Axel suggested. He knelt and put his arm around her shoulder and eased her upward.

The world swam. "Whoa."

"Take it easy, Dara." His voice was all concern. "Have a few sips. Call the ambulance, Murray."

"No! I can't afford it," she whispered. "I need the money for my baby." Canada might have free health care, but ambulance rides weren't covered.

"Call it. I'll pay for it."

Murray hurried off again.

"We need to make sure you didn't hurt the baby when you fell. I managed to catch you, but you went down hard."

"Okay," she said meekly, blinking back tears. *Why did he have to be so kind?* There was no way she could continue this charade. Which, of course, was exactly why she'd tried to get out of giving him the town tour. She fumbled to find her keys. "Can you drop my car at City Hall and leave the keys at the office?"

"I'll bring them to you at the hospital."

"Um. No. That's okay. You don't need to do that." *Would he just go away already?* Every time she looked in his stormy eyes, she wanted to confess. She did not want him to feel obligated to hang around. She didn't want to be part of his crazy lifestyle. She had had enough of that insanity as the daughter of a former low-level politician. The parties, the public events, the media. Thank heaven those days ended when her mother retired. She didn't want to go there again. If and when she married, it would be to a homebody like herself, not a superstar playboy jock.

"Until we talk, I'm not letting you out of my sight. The last time we were together, I fell asleep with you in my arms and didn't see you again for nearly nine months. If not for this arena thing, I'd never have found you."

"Whatever."

His lips turned up in what might have been a smirk, and he looked pointedly at her enormous belly. "Mine or not. I'm not finished with you."

The words came out like a soft, warm, welcoming threat. She shivered. *Dirty diapers! Did his blunt masculinity have to be so danged attractive?* Of course, that's why she'd slept with him in the first place.

The medics poured in. With lightning speed, they had her checked out, bundled up, and on her way to the hospital. She gave him one last look as they rolled her out the front door. For a second, she was sure she saw actual concern in his eyes.

·♥·♥·♥·♥·♥·

A xel broke a few speed records and managed to beat the ambulance to the hospital. Thank heaven for GPS. He was waiting inside when they rolled Dara through the emergency room doors. He followed the medics pushing the stretcher as if he belonged with her. As if he were a concerned husband.

"You don't need to be here," she hissed.

"I told you. I'm here until I know you're fine." *And until I find out if this baby is mine.*

"Honey," the gray-haired female medic said, "It's so sweet your man wants to stay with you. Many aren't so lucky." She patted Axel on the forearm. "Stick with her, son. She'll be scared and not want to admit it."

"I'll do that."

A young nurse in Christmas print scrubs came in and took a report from the medics, and they departed. She took Dara's vitals while questioning her about what happened. When Dara tried to push it off as nothing, he inserted himself into the conversation.

"She had a shock, and she fainted. I caught her, but she went down hard. We need to be sure both she and the baby are fine."

"Absolutely, sir." She gave him a flirtatious smile. "We'll take care of them both. Can I get you to come with me, and we'll do some paperwork?"

"We'll do it here." He handed Dara the sparkly purse she had forgotten earlier. She'd need her healthcare card. "Ask Dara your questions." He pulled a chair up to the bedside and grasped Dara's icy hand in his. "She's freezing. Is there a warm blanket?"

The nurse hurried away.

Dara glared at him before saying, "I *am* cold. Thanks."

The nurse came back, and he was forced to sit in the tastefully holiday-decorated hallway for an interminable forty-two minutes while they did their examination. Finally, he was called back in. He immediately sat, took Dara's hand in his, and turned his attention to the doctor.

"I'm Dr. Helman. Both mama and baby will be fine. Though we are going to induce her. She has preeclampsia. Her blood pressure is too high. The pregnancy is far enough along that it is safe to deliver the baby. It's better for them both."

Her fingers squeezed his hand until her nails dug in. He squeezed back and stroked her thumb with his until her grip lightened.

"What are the risks?" He asked when Dara didn't. His heart pounded.

The doctor went through a litany of possibilities, all of which terrified him. Dara grew whiter and whiter with each item he listed. *This was insane!*

"And if we don't induce?" He squeezed the question past the lump in his throat.

"The baby could suffer. She's in distress already."

"She?" *They were having a girl!?*

"Figure of speech. We prefer not to call the infant it, and Dara has said she doesn't wish to know the gender. Of course, she'll know soon enough."

"Do what's best for my baby. Please," Dara whispered, her voice shaking. She must be terrified. The entreaty in her words broke his heart.

The doctor explained the procedure to start labor, and finished by saying, "The room will be ready when she is. Are you coming into the delivery room?"

"No. Definitely not." He waved off the idea with both hands.

"It's proven that women with delivery support have babies that thrive better than those without." The doctor looked at him like he was lower than dirt.

"Don't you have a birthing coach, or partner, or whatever?" He asked. *He did not want to be there!*

"I do. My boss, my friend, Julia. I'll text her."

He was chased out of the room again while they did something to Dara. And four hours later, when they were ready to take her into delivery, her friend hadn't responded. They started to wheel her away, and she clutched his hand. "I can't do this alone," she whispered, fear making her voice tremble.

Holy hockey sticks! He couldn't go into the delivery room. No way. No how. Not even if they were married. He'd never be able to stand seeing her in that much pain. Even watching her up to this point had torn out his heart. He'd give up his mansion and sports cars, and do whatever he could, to take her pain away.

He opened his mouth to refuse. She squeezed his fingers and looked at him with watery eyes as another contraction rippled through her.

"Okay. I'll come." He wasn't a coward. He'd been sky diving, scuba diving, and he'd driven a Formula One car. He'd hunted, handled snakes, and survived a bar fight or two. He'd never been as terrified as he was at this moment.

Birth was gross, right? Bloody and messy? What if something happened to Dara or the baby? Could he handle that?

Jeez. This was a huge mistake.

Still, he'd given his word. Meekly, on weak knees, he followed the stretcher into a tiny room filled with machines and equipment. It looked like a science lab.

"If you're squeamish, Dad, stand facing Mom," a nurse in Santa-patterned scrubs advised. "You can keep your eyes away from the business end of things and still support her."

He huffed out a breath. *Thank heaven.* "I can do that." He took his place at her side, holding her hands. Or rather, letting her squeeze the life out of his. He was going to have bruises.

Several hours later, his nerves shot, and his feet aching, time suddenly vanished when the baby cried, and the doctor proclaimed, "It's a beautiful girl. Dad, would you like to cut the cord?"

He bit back a gag. "No, thanks."

"Are you sure? It's a real bonding moment. It ties everyone together as a family."

How could cutting a cord tie them together?

But, maybe binding her to him wasn't a bad idea. He had missed Dara from the moment he woke up to find her gone. He sucked in a breath and steeled his nerves. This day had been bad enough already. He turned slowly and said, "What do I do?"

·♥·♥·♥·♥·♥·

Chapter Four

Dara was astounded when Axel agreed to help with the delivery. But when he agreed to cut the cord, tears leaked down her cheeks.

It's just the emotion of delivery. Pregnancy hormones. He doesn't actually care about either of us. He felt obligated because he made me faint. She pushed the thoughts away and reached out for her baby girl. She was red and wrinkled and the most beautiful thing Dara had ever seen. She cuddled the baby against her naked breasts, uncaring that Axel was there. Skin-to-skin contact was crucial for bonding.

He stepped up and stroked their daughter's cheek. "She's beautiful, just like her mom. I'm so proud of you, Dara. You've done a difficult and beautiful thing. Thanks for bringing our daughter into the world safely." He caught her gaze.

Our baby. He knew.

Unable to vocalize the admission, she nodded in acknowledgment that the infant was his. He cleared his throat and blinked rapidly.

"I guess the mayor sent the right person," he teased. "I am definitely running my hockey school from Berry Cove." He winked.

"Are you mad at me?" *How could he not be furious?*

"Yes. But it doesn't matter. I found you again. I looked for you in every town and every bar I went to. Half a dozen times, I chased down a total stranger, thinking she could be you. I spent hours at the mall looking for you."

"You don't have to feel obligated to stay because of the baby."

"Even if there was no baby, I'd be staying anyway. For you."

Tears leaked from her eyes and ran down her cheeks. *Ugh. She was an emotional wreck.* She blinked furiously, not willing to release her hold on their baby. He turned around and grabbed a clean cloth from the counter behind him. Gently, he wiped her tears.

"No crying, beautiful. This is a joyous day. As soon as you're both up to it, we'll start house shopping."

"I have a house."

"I, *we*, do not."

She wasn't up to the argument. She closed her eyes and ignored him until the nurse said it was time to start nursing. "What will you call her?" the nurse asked.

"Jane. After my mom."

"Beautiful," Axel said. "If you don't mind, I'd like to add Elizabeth, for my mom."

"Jane Elizabeth. I like that." Their first compromise. It felt right.

He leaned in and kissed her cheek. "A beautiful name for a beautiful child. I have to run for a moment. Will you two be okay without me?"

He was leaving? Now?

"Don't worry," he said, obviously recognizing her distress. "I'll be back quickly."

She nodded, suddenly too tired and too overwhelmed to speak.

"She'll be in the maternity ward on the third floor when you come back. Just ask at the nursing station."

Jane was weighed and measured, then cleaned up. Her vitals were checked time and again. "Is she okay?"

"She's perfect," the pediatrician who had been part of the birthing team said. "Standard procedure to ensure she's in perfect health."

Some of the tension she'd felt since seeing Axel slid from Dara's shoulders, though she was certain he was gone for good. It was probably for the best if he left, but she was disappointed.

The nurse wheeled her into her new room. Her mouth dropped open. An enormous bouquet of roses and carnations sat on the nightstand, and an adorable dolphin stuffy sat on her pillow. Had he remembered her saying she loved dolphins? Surely not. She settled into the bed, rails up, baby in her arms, dolphin at her side, and tried not to be hurt that Axel wasn't there.

Her door whispered open. He came in without another sound, a large paper bag in one hand, a paper shopping bag dangling from its handles in the other. "Hey. I thought you might be asleep."

"No. Just resting a bit."

"You have to be so tired." He kissed her cheek. "I brought you something."

"What's that smell?" She inhaled deeply. Something deep fried. Her stomach rumbled. Her cheeks heated, but Axel just smiled.

"We've been here twelve hours. The nurses said you could eat whatever you want, as long as you stay hydrated. I brought dinner." He set the handled bag on the floor, just out of sight, and rolled her table over the bed and began pulling containers from the bag. "Chicken wings, sweet potato fries, bruschetta, deep-fried pickles, salad, and steak with a baked potato." He made a flourishing motion. "Pumpkin pie for dessert."

"That's enough to feed an army." She couldn't help but grin. She was ravenous.

"I thought we could share." He opened the containers and slid the steak onto a plastic plate. "I haven't eaten either."

Dinner was delicious. They ate in near silence, both transfixed by Baby Jane. He cleared up the empty containers. They'd eaten every bite. He urged her to drink.

"Now, for the best part." He set the second bag on the bed. "First this." He handed her an adorable onesie that said, Baby's First Christmas.

Suddenly overcome with emotion, she burst into tears.

"I can exchange it if you don't like it." His brow wrinkled in confusion.

She waved away his concern. "It's perfect," she said between sobs. She patted his hand. "Thank you." She sniffed. "I'm emotional because of the hormones and the birth. And you being here threw me for a loop."

"I didn't mean to mess things up for you." He pulled a small pre-decorated tree from the bag and set it on the windowsill. "It's a real tree," he said. "I thought we could plant it in our yard."

"Our yard?" *What was he thinking? That she'd marry him just because they shared this beautiful child? Hell no.* "I'm not marrying you."

"Dara, it might be our yard, as in me, you, and Jane. It might be the yard I only share with Jane, or *your* yard. It's a way to remember her first Christmas. I'll be there for you and Jane. Always. I need to be part of my daughter's, *our* daughter's, life. Even if I'm not part of yours, though I hope that eventually you'll fall for me."

Geez. She already had. Unable to speak over the conflicting emotions clogging her throat, she nodded. His relieved smile burned away a lot of her reservations.

"One more thing. Okay, a couple more." He handed her a small flat box. "Open it."

She pulled off the red ribbon and eased the top open. Inside lay an ornament. Three snowmen. A father, mother, and small child. It read, Our First Christmas, and had the year on the bottom.

"It's adorable."

"No matter what happens between you and me, we're family now." He handed her a jeweler's box. Ring-sized.

"I'm not marrying you."

"I don't recall asking."

Her heart dipped in disappointment. Almost as if she wanted a proposal.

"Open it. Please."

Her fingers trembled as she popped the box open to reveal a gold ring topped with two twisted hearts. A pretty red stone sat in the middle of the hearts. Maybe a ruby? It was lovely. She shook her head and pushed the box back at him.

"It's not an engagement ring. It's a promise ring. I promise to be there for you and Jane."

"You have a career. You live in Denver. I won't leave Berry Cove."

"That isn't a problem. I haven't told anyone yet, but at the end of the season, when my contract is up, I'm retiring. I'm tired of the travel, the parties, the daily workouts." He paused. "Okay, those will continue, but with less intensity. I've been planning this for two years. Hence, the hockey school. It will run year-round. The best part is that I've found you after months of looking and longing. We may not end up together, but at least now we have the chance to become friends, family, and maybe more. No rush, no pressure." He rested his hand atop hers, where it cradled Jane's tiny head. "I will be there for you." He slid the ring onto her right ring finger. It fit perfectly.

The door burst open, and Julia exploded in. "Oh my gosh," she exclaimed. "I'm sorry I couldn't come." She stopped dead. "What are you doing here?" She pointed at Axel. She looked at Dara. "Want me to throw him out?"

Dara giggled. "It's okay. We've worked things out. Sort of."

"I'm Axel Justice." He offered his hand.

"Julia Abrams." They shook.

"Well, Mayor Abrams. I will be having my lawyer write up a contract to use the arena on an ongoing basis. It will need an expansion, which I will provide as a donation to Berry Cove. Do you know any good real estate agents? I'm going to need a home here, to be close to my family."

Julia's stunned expression tickled a laugh out of Dara. She giggled. Somehow it became infectious, and Axel, then Julia, joined in.

"It's a Christmas miracle," Julia exclaimed.

"Yes, they are a Christmas miracle, aren't they?" Axel smiled down at Jane and Dara with sweet tenderness. Happiness bloomed in Dara's heart.

She smiled up at him. She already loved him. She had loved him from the moment they met. She would marry him, but not before they knew each other better. His rogue grin said he knew they were destined to be together, and she was fine with his smugness. This time.

"You two are the best Christmas present ever." He sat on the bed and pulled her into his arms for a sweet, deep kiss.

Epilogue

January 4th.

Dara stared at the house as she climbed out of the car. "This isn't at all what I expected."

"What were you expecting, a mansion?"

"Well, sort of." She shrugged as she watched Axel lift Jane and her carrier out of the backseat of his sensible SUV.

Axel laughed. "I knew you wouldn't want Jane living in a mansion, so I bought this." He waved toward the two-story house. It was fully decorated, though Christmas was long past. There was a large elm tree with a swing in the front yard, and a padded two-person swing on the front porch.

'It's pretty. But, I'm still annoyed that you wouldn't help me house shop." There was no heat in her voice.

"After you." He gestured her toward the front door.

She walked up the freshly shoveled sidewalk and onto the wooden porch.

"Go ahead, it's open."

She stepped inside and froze. It was beautiful. "It's lovely." She turned to face him.

"Thank heaven. I was worried I might screw it up. I tried to make it look like your place. I want you to be comfortable here. If there's anything you don't like, we can change it." He set the carrier on the plush mat and took Dara's jacket. He hung it on the elaborate, white wooden coat rack. "Come, I want to show you Jane's room."

She tried not to gawk at the other rooms when she passed, but couldn't help herself. Everything was perfect, exactly how she'd have decorated. It was like he'd taken her small house, and expanded it. He pushed open the door to Jane's room and waved her inside.

The walls were a soft blush pink and decorated with baby farm animals. The crib, change table, and dresser were white with gold trim. There was a matching rocker in the corner beside a small table. It was perfect.

Her knees went weak, and she hurried to the chair and dropped into it. "It's beautiful."

He placed Jane in her arms. "I'm glad you like it."

He knelt in front of her. "I know you said you won't marry me, but I want to be a father to Jane, and I need to be there for you both. At all times. Dara, you stole my heart on our first night together. I can't live without you. I can't help myself; I have to ask. Will you make me the world's happiest man? Will you marry me and make me complete?"

She blinked away tears of joy. "Oh, Axel," she whispered. "Yes, I will."

· ❤ · ❤ · ❤ · ❤ · ❤ ·

Healing Hearts

Chapter One

December twentieth. Four days until Christmas Eve. Another night alone. Still single. At least she could enjoy tonight. Jacinda looked around the Berry Cove Community Center, where the Christmas dance was in full swing.

Mayor Julia Abrams and her new husband, Neil Buch, danced the jive inside a circle of watching celebrants. Jarod and Tamara Ribbons stood chatting with Dara and Axel Justice. All her friends were paired up. Everyone except her.

Even all six of her exes were snuggled up with someone. Here she was, thirty-seven and alone. Still. But...her life was good, and she had no regrets.

Okay, maybe one. Or two.

And her biggest regret ever, Murray Ratcliff, stood laughing with a group of his friends. She tried not to stare at him as he enjoyed their company.

She wasn't alone, she was with Gabriella and Naomi. Though, at times, loneliness trickled in despite the festive party they were at.

Both of her friends looked beautiful in their holiday dresses. What a blast it had been to shop for dresses together. Naomi's was a beautiful green velvet with tight sleeves and a flowing hemline. Gabriella's, or Ella as she preferred to be called, was sinful red silk. Jacinda had settled on a floaty black number highlighted with sparkling black jewels. But it was Murray that caught her eye over and over again.

Lord, those broad shoulders, and lean hips. He'd been an under-appreciated teen when they dated, but now, the ex-soldier was too hot to resist. He was a heartbreaker for sure.

"Stop staring at him," Ella hissed.

"I'm not staring." She looked away. Guilty heat flooded her face.

"You are," Naomi countered. "Either go ask him out or quit staring. He's danced with everyone else. Why not you?"

"Oh, my God. You don't know?" Ella stared at Naomi.

"Know what?"

"Hush," Jacinda glared at her childhood friend. "Nobody else needs to know."

Naomi laughed. "Oh, this is rich. I thought I knew all your secrets." She turned to Ella. "Are you saying they used to date?" Naomi had only been in town a couple of years, and the disaster between Jacinda and Murray was nearly two decades ago.

Ella stepped closer and whispered. "They did. For nine months in grade twelve. He was a total nerd. She dumped him for the quarterback." She paused dramatically. "On prom night."

"No way. She'd never." She stared at Jacinda.

"I would. I did. Water under the bridge." She made a wavy motion with her hand as if it didn't matter. But it did. Too much. She'd been an idiot.

"And he hates you?"

"That's the thing," Ella said, "I don't think he does. She just won't talk to him. She'll go miles out of her way to avoid him."

"I do not!"

"She does."

Would this conversation never end? Maybe she could escape to the bathroom. "Look, over there, it's Vince. You should dance with him, Ella."

"Me? Dance with Vince? Not in this lifetime. That Lothario can kiss my Christmas holly."

The squeal of a microphone cut off any response Jacinda would have made. Mayor Abrams, who hadn't taken her husband's name, began announcing the door prize winners.

·♥·♥·♥·♥·♥·

M urray shifted on his aching feet and straightened his tie. *Why in the world am I even here?* There was nobody he wanted to dance with. He should never have let Vince and Mark convince him to come. Just because they were on the prowl didn't mean he was. That ship had sailed. He was nearly forty. Far too old to be thinking about a relationship and a family.

He'd only ever really wanted one woman, and she'd thrown him over for a jock. *A freaking jock!* He pushed out a breath. Years ago, he'd forgiven her. Her betrayal had hurt then. It still did. But he'd learned to let her go...mostly. Though he still wanted her, he'd abide by her decision, not that he had a choice. He just wanted her to be happy.

"Come on, Murray. Be my wingman. I'm going to ask Naomi to dance," Mark said.

"Because you didn't learn your lesson when she slapped you at the Valentine's dance?" Vince quipped.

Mark shrugged. "Things change. I'll wear her down."

"Well, I'm not going with you," Murray said. "I'm not dancing. I'm having another beer and heading home."

Across the hall, Jacinda's head tipped back and she laughed. He couldn't hear it from where he stood, but his traitorous memory was happy to fill in the sound. He swallowed a lump of melancholy. Her floaty dress sparkled in the twinkling fairy lights. She looked like a goddess with her blonde hair piled high and those sexy curves. She looked better now than she had in high school.

Screw the beer.

Christmas might be a time for family and friends, but if you had unrequited love, it totally sucked tinsel. "Never mind the beer. I'm out." No way could he stay and watch her having fun. Even after all these years, it stung. He shouldn't want Jacinda, but he did.

·♥·♥·♥·♥·♥·

Chapter Two

After her last charge drove away with his father, Jacinda glared at the black SUV in front of her daycare. Murray Ratcliff. Why did he have to own the house next door? And why was he parked in front of her place? The spot in front of his house was empty, and he had a parking spot out back, just like she did.

It's like fate was taunting her for a mistake she made two decades ago. She closed the blinds and switched off the Christmas tree. Strolling through the large bungalow that used to be her family home, she checked all the lights, locks, plugs, windows, and appliances. Everything was secure for the weekend. She could go home and put her feet up. She peeked through the glass panel beside the back door. The coast was clear.

She stepped out, locked up, and bolted for her car. She slid inside and turned the key.

Click. Click.

She winced. She really needed to get it to the garage for a new battery, but there never seemed to be enough time. *So much for a do-nothing weekend.*

Grabbing her laptop bag and purse, she got back out.

"Need a hand?"

She whirled toward her nemesis. "Don't do that! Ratcliff, you scared me right into next year!"

"Sorry. Won't start again?" He leaned on his shovel. How had she missed seeing him when she peeked out?

Oh, tinsel on toast, he'd shoveled around her car. Why did he have to be sweet? And how hadn't she noticed before getting in? She didn't deserve it after what she'd done to him. Still, he was always nice.

"I can probably fix that."

"I'll walk home and call the garage. Thanks."

"Jacinda, why do you push me away? We could be friends." His voice was heavy with hurt.

Ya, right. He was just trying to warm her up so he could repay her for the horrid way she'd dumped him. "I'm not pushing you away."

"You haven't said a dozen words to me in ten years. And in the ten before that, total radio silence. We used to be close."

"Fine. You can fix it," she said ungraciously.

"There's the girl I fell for in high school. Beauty and snark all rolled into one hot package. Let me get my tools." He headed for his garage.

Hot? He thought she was hot.

Guilt wracked her heart. She'd fallen for him back then, too. But in a bid to join the popular crew, she dumped him for the quarterback the morning of prom. She'd been such a witch. Karma had slapped her down when the jock dumped her, days later, for the head cheerleader, whom he'd been dating before Jacinda.

Then, Murray, the high school nerd and chess champion, had left town, joined the army, and returned a war hero. He became her ideal man, and she couldn't have him. The quarterback had cheated on his taxes and business partners and ended up in jail for forgery and embezzlement. Karma was a witch.

Murray was back in two minutes, tools in hand. He could fix literally anything, and that was why Berry Cove had hired him to manage their arena and sports complex.

Light snow dusted his dark hair and lingered on the collar of his sheepskin-lined denim jacket. His dark-rimmed glasses gave him the nerdy look she'd adored when they dated. His broad shoulders told of his time in the service. The combination was lethal to her heart and hormones.

She popped the hood, and he pulled out some kind of gizmo with a screen and connected it to the battery. "Your battery is dead. What happened? This is a fairly new car."

"I don't know. I went to Hawaii for a week, and when I came back, nothing. I think the interior light was on. I charged it, but it doesn't stay charged."

"You didn't leave it plugged in? It was minus forty for five days. You probably froze the battery. A new battery will fix it right up. Come on, I'll take you to the parts store."

"Are you sure that's what it is?" She didn't have a whole lot of extra money after her trip.

"There could be more wrong, but I'm betting a battery will fix everything. If not, I'll help you find the cause."

More than anything, she wanted to ask why he was being so kind to someone who had done him so wrong. "I would appreciate the help, but you really don't have to."

"It's no problem. Come on, my SUV is warm. I just got in from work. We'll have your car fixed up in no time."

Karma was not smiling on her because the parts store had to order a new battery for her. It wouldn't be in until after Boxing Day, the twenty-sixth. She was on foot until then.

"I'll run you home. I can pick you up tomorrow if you need to go anywhere, and for work on Monday. It's dipping down to minus thirty-six tonight. That would be a cold walk."

"It's only a few blocks."

"It's at least fifteen, and I'll be up anyway. No arguments. I'll be there at quarter to six."

She gaped at him. *How did he know what time she got to work?* "Thanks. I appreciate it." She really didn't want to walk in the bitter cold.

Snow drifted down on them as he headed out of the parking lot. "I can't believe it's snowing and going to get so cold overnight."

"Cold fronts will do that. At least it won't last beyond the weekend. It'll be nice by Christmas Eve. Did you need groceries or anything for the weekend? I need some myself."

"I could grab a couple of things, if you don't mind stopping." She could grab a bottle of wine and some snacks.

"No problem." He drove slowly down the street. "Wow, it's getting dicey out here. It's really coming down."

"I'll be fast in the store."

They hurried through the thick falling snow and inside. "I'll race you to the register," he challenged as they stomped off their boots.

"You're on." She grabbed a cart and bolted toward the snack aisle. A few snacks, some cheese, some wine, and she'd be set for the weekend. The race was nostalgic. They'd done this often while dating. Who could get their errands done the fastest? Or their homework. Of course, he usually won that one. She wasn't stupid, but she couldn't hold a candle to his amazing intelligence.

When she got to the front, he was already there, with three bags of groceries in his cart. "How'd you do that so fast?"

The cashier laughed. "He ordered online. He cheated." The fifty-ish cashier laughed. "I can't believe you two still play that game. You really are well suited to each other."

"We're not together," she corrected, even as he replied, "We sure are."

"Oh. I see," her tone suggesting otherwise. She rang up Jacinda's order, quickly bagging the items while she chatted.

Outside, visibility had fallen to near zero.

"Holy crap. This is awful." Working together, they cleared off his SUV. "I'll skip hitting the liquor store. Maybe you should just drop me off at the daycare. I can stay there. No sense going all the way to my place and back. Thirty blocks in this weather is taking too much risk." She grasped his arm. "I don't want to put either of us in danger."

"You have food at the daycare?"

"Yes." She said, somewhat sarcastically. "I do feed my charges, you know."

"Of course, I wasn't thinking." He focused on the road. After two blocks, he said, "Why don't you stay with me. I've got a fireplace. Just in case the power goes out, or we lose heat."

She shivered despite the warm air blowing from the air vents. She hated power outages. Especially in the winter. Too many bad memories.

"If you don't mind."

·❤·❤·❤·❤·❤·

Chapter Three

Murray's nerves were stretched to breaking by the time they made it home. The snowplows weren't out yet, and almost nobody was on the road. He was grateful that he lived so close to Main Street. The walkway he'd shoveled earlier was ankle deep in snow.

"You're going to get wet feet," he warned. She wore running shoes. In the dead of winter. *Insane.*

"My shoes will dry." She hopped out and grabbed half of the bags from the backseat. He hurried to catch up with the rest as she waited on his back deck.

"I love this deck," she said. The deck took up a full third of the yard and was festooned with white fairy lights.

"First thing I put in after Mom and Dad moved to Arizona and I bought their house. I'm not much for lawn mowing. Less grass is better. The door's unlocked." He reached past her and opened the screen door. She opened the inner door. Locking doors wasn't really a Berry Cove thing.

Blessedly warm air swept over them as he flipped a switch, and the lights came on.

"Oh, this is so nice. I thought it was warm in the car. Apparently not." She laughed and rubbed her cold hands together.

The sound was sweet, hot, honey running down his spine. As a teen, that laugh was the biggest imaginable aphrodisiac. Even now, it made his heart jumpy. "I'll turn up the heat." Boots off, he dropped his bags in the kitchen and hurried to the living room. He flipped on the tree and turned up the heat.

"The tree's lovely and it smells heavenly."

"I always get a real tree. I'm looking into a living tree for next year. Of course, this one was from Updike's Tree Farm, so it was grown for this purpose. When I take it back, they'll mulch it and sell the mulch next summer."

"What a lovely idea." Her gaze was everywhere. The new hardwood flooring, the fireplace, the comfortable furnishings, the art on the walls. "Wow. It's changed a lot in here. I love it."

Her praise was nice. "Thanks. I've updated a bit over the years. My favorite is the kitchen. Mom loved the granite counters when they were home last summer."

"Oh, show me. I'm thinking of granite when I upgrade."

She admired the kitchen as they put away the groceries. "I could use some dinner. How about you?" She tilted her head to look up at him.

"Sure. Let me whip up something." With a click, all the lights went out.

"Oh," she squeaked. "I guess that means no cooking." Her voice trembled.

He laughed. "Gas stove."

"Awesome." Her voice trembled, but still held relief.

"But first, I'll start a fire. It'll cool off quickly in here, even though I had the house wrapped for better insulation when I did the upgrades."

· ❤ · ❤ · ❤ · ❤ · ❤ ·

Not wanting to be alone in the dark, she followed him to the living room and watched him work. He was graceful and less clumsy than he had been years ago. Military training must have helped with that. He was being so kind to her and looking after her needs. She realized he always had. Obviously, he didn't hold a grudge over her dumping him on prom night.

They talked about nothing while he cooked and while they ate. Finally, she had to know why he didn't hate her. "Why are you even talking to me?"

"Why wouldn't I? We grew up together, right in these two houses. Your daycare is next door. We've known each other for years." He seemed genuinely confused as he placed a few more candles around the living room and lit them.

"I dumped you. On prom night. After nine months of dating. It was a witchy thing to do." Cinnamon and cranberry scents drifted through the room. "I don't understand why you even talk to me."

"You forget that we told each other everything. All our hopes and fears. How you wanted to be a mother more than anything else. How you didn't understand why society frowns on non-working mothers? How it bothered you that the "in" crowd snubbed you just because you wore metal braces and not invisible ones."

He was quiet for a moment and then said, "I understood why you went with him. I know your heart."

She nearly swooned at his words. So romantic. Unable to speak past the lump in her throat, she nodded for him to go on. Listening to him talk kept her fears of the storm at bay.

He sat beside her on the couch and clasped her hand in his. "I was angry. Then he dumped you days later. You floundered. I was too upset and hurt to go to you and offer comfort. I should have. Mom wanted to have you over that Christmas. I refused." He laughed wryly. "Boy, did I get an earful."

"Why?"

"Mom gave me the 'Christmas is a time for love, joy, and forgiveness' speech. And the one about how I should be glad to have had any time with you. She really made me think."

"I don't understand."

"I might have been a stupid kid, but I realized that I did still love you. I wanted your happiness more than anything else. If that meant you being with the "in crowd", and not with me, I was happy with it." He chuckled again. "Maybe not happy, but you get the idea."

"You're a better person than I am. I'd still be mad."

"No, Jacinda, you wouldn't be. You'd have forgiven me. Maybe not enough to take me back, but enough to wish me well."

He had no idea. She would have been mad. No way she'd be able to forgive what she'd done to him if it happened in reverse. "Why didn't you ask me out again?"

"I thought about it. The timing never seemed right. I dated a bit and wouldn't ask you out while I was seeing someone else. And when I was free, you weren't. It wasn't our time."

What did that mean? Not their time?

Outside, something thumped.

"What was that?" She leaped to her feet and looked around.

·❤·❤·❤·❤·❤·

Murray watched her. Something was wrong. She seemed scared. "It sounded like snow sliding off the roof." He kept his voice calm and soothing.

Her arms were wrapped around her middle, and she was chewing her lip. That was the scared Jacinda. "I'll look. Hang tight." He pulled back the curtain and stared out into total darkness.

"What was it?" She gripped his arm from behind.

"I don't see anything. I'll check out back." He threaded their fingers together and tugged her after him. He shone the flashlight of his phone out the window. "Look at the pile of snow under that spruce. I'll bet that's what we heard. Nothing to worry about."

"Okay, if you're sure." She didn't sound convinced.

"Come on, back to the fireplace and heat." She stayed so close that her entire side rubbed against him. She barely let him get through the doorway without her. "I love a crackling fire." He opened the glass doors, threw in a few logs, and slid them shut again.

She stayed right at his elbow. Yup, definitely scared. He spread a quilt in front of the fire. "Remember how we used to lie?"

·❤·❤·❤·❤·❤·

Chapter Four

J acinda managed a laugh. "Head-to-head." Close enough to kiss but not to touch easily. It helped keep their hormones contained. Aside from dumping him, missing the chance to make love with Murray was her biggest regret.

He lay down by the fire with enough space for her to lie in her usual position. "I can't believe you remembered that," she said and lay down with him. His feet facing east, hers facing west.

"Jacinda, I remember every minute we spent together. Every. Single. One."

By rolling up on one elbow, they were able to sip wine in the candlelight. The alcohol and his presence soothed her fear.

"Feeling better?"

"What?" She pretended not to understand.

"You seemed nervous. Were you afraid?"

"No."

"Liar," he said softly. "I know you, Jacinda. You were scared. Want to talk about it?"

Why did he have to be so understanding? How could she keep her distance when he was so nice? It was why she'd avoided him since their breakup. She sat up, wrapped her arms around her legs, and stared into the fire.

"You don't have to tell me." His voice held the same compassion he'd shown her years ago when she was upset or flustered over something she wasn't ready to share with him.

"I was six." She sniffed back a tear. "We were at Grams and Gramps's cabin for a winter camp. It was fun."

"Until it wasn't?"

"Yeah." He shifted and stroked his hand down her back. The touch was soothing. "Everyone went for a night toboggan run. Except me. I had a cold and wanted to stay inside. Mom let me because they wouldn't be long." Memories swirled over her, stealing her breath. Tears welled in her eyes. She wiped them away.

"What happened, Jacinda?" He slid behind her, one leg on either side, and wrapped his arms around her waist the way he used to. The familiar position felt good. Too good. But she didn't shift away.

She took a deep breath before speaking. "They hadn't lit a fire yet. No way they'd leave a kid alone with a fire. Even in the fireplace. I don't know what caused it, but minutes after they left, the power went out." She shuddered. "I promised not to leave the house. I promised. But it was dark. So dark." She swallowed hard. "I got dressed to go outside and find them, but it was darker outside. I didn't know where the hill was. I couldn't remember. So, I went back inside. It seemed like hours until they came back. The house made stupid noises. I was freezing."

"Jeez. That's awful. No wonder you're nervous now." He rubbed her shoulders and then wrapped his arms back around her waist. "You never told me."

"I never told anyone. I still sleep with a nightlight."

"I'll bet it's shaped like a starfish."

She chuckled. "How did you know?"

"Starfish earrings. Starfish shirt. That starfish pendant you always wear. You did your final biology paper on starfish." He was quiet for a moment. "I know you, Jacinda."

"Apparently."

"Do you want more candles? I have plenty."

"No, I'm okay. A guy with candles?" *What did a single man need candles for, except for romancing women? Was he dating that much? Had she missed it?*

"I was a soldier. I've got a prepper mindset. Candles, oil lamps. M.R.E.s."

"M.R. whatsits?"

"M.R.E.s. Meals, ready-to-eat. Survival rations. I make them myself. Twenty years shelf stable."

She loved the pride in his voice. "I guess I'm stranded with the right man." She might be afraid, but she was glad to be with him. Finally. She shifted back to lie on the rug, just out of reach of his tempting body. As much as she wanted to lean into his body, she couldn't go there. Couldn't allow herself the comfort and temptation of his body.

"I'm sorry," she said an hour and two glasses of wine later. She turned toward him, rolling up on one elbow. He rolled toward her.

"For what? For being afraid? No apology necessary."

"For dumping you. It was a rotten thing to do."

"Apology accepted. But only if you forgive yourself."

He stroked his finger down her cheek. She shivered.

"Jacinda," he whispered, "Will you go out with me?" His breath caressed her cheek.

She looked deep into his eyes. *Was he serious? He couldn't be.* He looked serious.

"Will you give me the chance to prove I'm worthy?"

She frowned. "Murray, you were always worthy. I wasn't worthy of you." She shifted self-consciously, and their fingers met. He interlaced them, and she didn't have the strength to pull away.

"Look at us. Same problem. Different sides of the same coin."

She stared at him for longer than she should. Lord, she missed him. For two decades, she'd watched him. Wanted him. Never once did she think he'd be open to the emotional intimacy they were sharing.

"Do you know how hard it is to watch you come and go next door? Every single day. It about rips my heart out. I've had so many imaginary conversations with you. When I got a promotion, when I graduated bootcamp, when I got the rink job, when something exciting happened, *you* were the one I wanted to call. I dream about being with you."

"Oh, Murray." He was so sweet. "I do know. More than you'll ever know." There was a quiet intimacy in the darkness that made secret sharing easier. "I wanted to rip the hair out of every woman who dated you."

"You always were a bit jealous."

"Ya. Zero self-confidence."

· ♥ · ♥ · ♥ · ♥ · ♥ ·

Murray considered her words. "I never would have guessed that. Maybe I don't know you as well as I thought." He wished she were still in his arms. He'd missed holding her all those years. Now that he had a fresh taste, he never wanted it to end.

"Do we ever really know anybody?"

He couldn't see her expression as clearly as he wanted. He needed to read her eyes. "Ask me anything. I'll answer truthfully. I have no secrets from you."

She snorted a laugh. "What was it like dating Betsy Franklin?"

Big Boobs Betsy, they called her in high school. Everyone wanted to be with her. Even Murray. "Honestly? They were the worst three dates of my life." He chuckled. "She's nice, but she's not exactly a deep thinker. She relied fully on her body to get by. I always wondered why the guys bragged about being with her, but nobody stuck with her. I sure found out. She's a server in a bar in Grande Prairie now."

Silence fell for a few minutes, then he asked, "What was it like dating Gibson Henderson?" If he was going to confess to anything that she asked, he was getting in some questions of his own.

"Rather a lot like Betsy, I suspect. He was all hands. They probably would have made a good pair." She slapped a hand over her mouth. "That was rude. I try not to disparage anyone." He didn't say anything else, so she asked, "What are you afraid of?"

"Nuclear war. Government despots. Environmental disasters ruining the food chain. Toxic chemicals being sprayed on our food."

"Be serious."

"I am. Fully, one hundred percent, serious."

"Okay, on a more personal level."

A candle flickered and went out. Jacinda didn't seem to notice it, but he got up and lit another one anyway. He took a seat on the edge of a chair. "Honest to Christmas? I'm scared to death that when the power comes on and the roads are passable that you'll walk out that door and never talk to me again."

She gasped and bolted upright. "Don't mess with me, Murray."

He walked over to her and cupped her chin in his hands. "With one complete honesty, on the joy of Christmas, and by all that is holy, having you here is the best thing that's happened to me since you walked out of my life nineteen years, one hundred ninety-seven days, twelve hours, and a handful of minutes ago. Not that I'm counting."

He shifted left, bringing her face into the light. Her eyes were misty; her mouth parted in a shocked half smile. Tempting. Too tempting. With the crackling fire, the quiet darkness, and the candles, the entire evening was romantic and begged him to have more from her. More for *them*.

"I'm going to kiss you, Jacinda."

She nodded and licked her lips.

He swept in and tasted her. Sweet white wine and the beautiful flavor that was uniquely Jacinda, and the stuff of dreams. He stepped back a half step. "I never stopped loving you." He turned and walked into the kitchen, leaving her there alone.

· ❦ · ❦ · ❦ · ❦ · ❦ ·

O *h no, he didn't.* She stormed after him, grabbed his shoulder, and spun him around.

"You do not get to drop a bombshell like that and walk away, Murray Ratcliff. No way." She grabbed him and yanked him to her. Their chests met, and she snuggled closer. "I've wanted you way too long to let you get away with just one kiss."

She crushed her lips against his and was instantly lost to the heat and passion sparking between them. His arms slid around her waist, pulling her closer, leaning her backwards. He pressed down against her and pulled her toward him. Her heart soared, and her soul felt at peace. *Holy Christmas! This was where she belonged. Right here. In his arms.*

The kiss went on forever and was over in an instant. She pulled back and leaned her forehead against his chest. "Holy Mistletoe! You sure can kiss."

His chest rumbled with laughter. "I could say the same about you." He kissed the top of her head. "Jacinda, Jacinda. What am I going to do with you?"

"I figure you could kiss me again. You know, just to make sure the punch of that last one wasn't just a one-off thing."

"Happy to oblige."

Several minutes later, they broke apart. "As much fun as this is," he panted, "I think we should go somewhere warmer. You'll freeze out here. Back to the fire you go. I'll be right there."

She snuggled in front of the fire, listening to him rummage in the kitchen. She missed him already. He came in with a bottle of cinnamon schnapps, a camping kettle, a container of Jiffy Pop, and some other things on a tray.

"Snack time. Want some hot cocoa?"

"I'd rather have another kiss." She winked, though she wasn't kidding in the least.

He set the tray on the table and knelt before her. "One more kiss. Then no more. Not until we've had an official date. I don't go about kissing girls I'm not dating. Except my ninety-two-year-old grandmother."

Her heart jumped. "Are you asking me out?"

"Yes."

He brushed his lips over hers, and the room flooded with light. It took her a full minute to realize the power was back on.

"The power's on!" she nearly shouted.

"Bummer. I kind of liked having you all to myself in the dark."

She got up and shut off all the lights except the tree. "Will that do?"

"Will you date me?" he countered.

"I thought you'd never ask. Yes, Murray Ratcliff, I will date you."

He grabbed her arm and fell back onto the couch, pulling her on top of him. "Well then, Jacinda Jones, you may have another kiss."

She brushed her lips across his. "What do you want for Christmas, Murray?" At this point, all she wanted was to kiss him, but she also wanted to go slow.

"Just this. Just you. One date and a chance for the future. Merry early Christmas, Jacinda."

"Merry Christmas, Murray."

Their lips met, and reality swirled away in a rush of joy.

·♥·♥·♥·♥·♥·

Forgive and Forget

Chapter One

"Welcome to the Berry Hills Elementary PTA meeting," Principal Brewer welcomed the staff and parents. "Tonight, we'll finalize plans for the Christmas concert."

Gabriella Ryan, Ella to those closest to her, leaned to her best friend, Naomi, and whispered, "It's only October. Why are we doing this now? And why on a Friday with thirty minutes' notice?"

"Miss Ryan, is there something you'd like to share with the group?" Brewer pinned her with a stare. He was the most intense, no-nonsense person she'd ever met.

"Just saying how excited I am for the concert. The grade threes will be ready to go." Ella barely resisted the urge to roll her eyes.

"See that they are. On that note, I'm assigning you the task of talking to the owner of La Torta and securing a discount for the desserts we'll need. I have a list."

She gaped at him for a moment and snapped her mouth shut. Across the room, the fourth-grade teacher grumbled her disagreement. Muriel had a massive crush on Vince Marino, the owner of La Torta, the local Italian bakery. Ella, on the other hand, would rather walk over a mile of ice shards at minus forty, barefoot, than talk to that conniving cheater ever again. Beside her, her friend, Jacinda, snorted a laugh.

Jacinda leaned in to whisper. "Fate. Fate wants you and Vince back together."

Easy for her to say, she was happily engaged and off the market, and she hadn't been burned by Vince's Lothario ways.

"I want you to take this list and have a quote by Tuesday." His smile was vindictive. He thrust the list in her direction, just far enough out of reach that she had to get up to take it from him.

Naomi jabbed her with an elbow when she sat back down. "He's just pissed that you won staff of the month three times in a row, and he hasn't won since he got here, three years ago."

While she appreciated the recognition, the award was nothing more than a popularity contest with students and parents. And since she worked on the yearbook committee, the dance committee, and the story-maker's club, her name was easy to recognize when the vote went online. It was a simple matter of her working with a greater number of students than the other teachers.

"Shh," she hissed at Naomi. "I ran the whole event last year. I don't want to do it again, and he's just vindictive enough to dump it all on me."

Brewer glared in their direction, his brows dipping down, making his chubby cheeks look puffier. He had the perfect round body to portray Santa, but he sure didn't have the jolly demeanor or the giving heart.

"We could use another bakery, or split the purchases between several," she suggested.

"La Torte is our tradition. It has been since I began at this school. We're sticking with it."

Resisting the urge to argue, Ella leaned back and rolled her eyes. The meeting dragged on and on. It was nearly eight thirty when it finally broke up. Brewer stormed over and tapped the list. "Remember, numbers by Tuesday."

"It's Friday," she protested.

"That's four days, five if you count Tuesday." Pivoting on his heel, he stormed off.

"It's a darn good thing the bakery is on my way home. I guess I'll skip drinks tonight. We'll catch up on Monday. We can talk about the Christmas games next week." Naomi and Jacinda had volunteered to be part of the games committee, despite not having any children. Technically, neither should have been at the meeting, but they'd been at the school to pick her up for their night out when Brewer announced his impromptu meeting.

After warm hugs between the three of them, she headed out. It was seventeen blocks to the bakery, and another three to her apartment. At least she could reward herself for the walk. La Torte had some of the best desserts in town, and their biscotti was to die for.

"Maybe I'll get lucky," she muttered as she bundled up against the cold. "Maybe his manager will be in, and I won't have to deal with Vince."

La Torte's door chimed brightly as she entered. She stomped snow off her boots and looked up. Right into Vince Marino's eyes. *Glitter and gluey fingers.*

His expression went from startled to pure welcome. "Ella, come in. Come in. Let me get you a latte to warm you up. Cinnamon dolce, right?" His dark brown eyes sparkled.

"Um. Ya. *" How did he know her order?*

"And a pistachio biscotti?"

"Yes, please." She hesitated, a bit thrown off by his eager welcome. "How's your mom?"

"Fit as a fiddle. She's loving being in the seniors' apartments. Her social life is booming. She's really blossomed since moving in."

"I'm glad. She was so lonely after your father passed."

"Ya. She was." Looking sad, he strode behind the counter, and for a moment, they didn't speak. The noise of the brewer was too overwhelming. "What brings you in? I don't usually see you this late in the day." He slid her latte across the counter.

"The school Christmas concert."

"What, no Muriel Abberford this year?"

"She does like you," she teased. Muriel and Vince went way back, and one thing was certain: Vince had no interest in anyone who chased after him like he was a veal cutlet, especially Muriel, who'd been a thorn in his side since the day he started high school. When Vince and Ella dated, he used to complain about Muriel's persistence.

"Don't go there." He shook his finger at her.

"You seemed to like her in grade twelve," she snapped, unable to squelch her hurt.

"Don't go there," he repeated with a low growl. "This is the last time I'm going to tell you. I did not kiss Muriel Abberford. Not even once."

"I saw you, Vince. With my own eyes."

"She kissed me."

"Same damned thing."

"No. It isn't. And she tasted like death. Honestly, she had the worst coffee breath I've ever smelled. I had no interest in her. I never have and I never will. She's a nice enough person; she just isn't *my* person." He slammed a biscotti on a plate and turned away. "It's on the house."

She stared at his broad shoulders as he strode into the kitchen. He'd filled out so much since they dated the last time. She was a sucker for his delicious Italian looks and that accent. Holy Christmas crackers, it made her knees weak. His Italian family had arrived in Berry Cove by way of South Africa. His accent was a sexy blend of both places. They'd opened the bakery when he was in tenth grade. She'd thought he would lose the accent, sound more Canadian, but it had stuck fast.

"Don't you walk away from me," she demanded.

The teenage employee who was working quietly in the corner stared. Her eyes went wide, and her mouth dropped open. She'd probably never heard anyone yell at her boss before.

Ella stomped past her to follow him. "Vince Marino, I want to talk to you." She pushed her way around the pastry chef and into Vince's office, sliding in just before he would have slammed the door.

"That's just it, Gabriella Ryan, you don't want to talk. Talking implies a conversation. You're just stuck on your anger and refuse to listen. I'm sick to death of it. Grow the F up. Send someone else with the Christmas list, because if I have to deal with you, I won't do the baking."

Holy cow!

She had to do this. Brewer had the power to fire her. Her brain went fuzzy, and she dropped into a chair.

·♥·♥·♥·♥·♥·

Vince raced to Ella's side. "Hey, take it easy. Are you okay?" Being a natural redhead, she was always on the pale side, but right now, she was sheet white. Pale, ghostly white. Her pretty green eyes seemed unfocused.

She pushed him away. "I'm fine. Not that it matters to you."

"What does that mean?" He was tired of this constant arguing. It had been eighteen years since the Muriel incident. "Come on, Ella. I don't want to fight with you. We had something special once. Can't we at least be friends?"

Her entire body shook with her sigh. When she looked up at him, her eyes shone with unshed tears. "I...I don't think so."

He pulled another chair so he could sit across from her in the tiny space between the door and his desk. He clasped her hands in his. "Can we at least stop being enemies?" He squeezed her fingers. "Talk to me."

"Brewer hates me." She sucked in a breath and pushed it out.

Sweet memories exploded over him. She still smelled like peppermints and strawberry lip gloss.

"He has the power to have me transferred out of his school. Out of Berry Cove. I've lived here my entire life. I don't want to live anywhere else. He could go beyond an involuntary transfer. He could...he could fire me." Her voice trembled.

"The rest of the world isn't so bad," Vince tried to commiserate. Her frown made his stomach ache. "You survived university. And there are dozens of small Alberta towns in need of a great teacher."

"You don't understand. I just need to keep this job, and he detests me. I feel like a damned teenager, always on edge when he's around. Waiting for something bad to happen."

"Why does he dislike you?" *How could anyone dislike his Ella?*

"I have no idea why he dislikes me. Just guesses. We butted heads the first week he was here. He wanted to cancel Story Writers. I threatened to teach it out of my house if he did. The parents kicked up a fuss. Now, I've won teacher of the month several months in a row, and he's not happy."

"He might win it if he weren't so grumpy." Brewer came in for coffee five days a week and never smiled or thanked the staff. Not even once.

"Please work with me on this." She sniffed. "I don't want to lose my job."

Could he stand to work with her? It would mean half a dozen meetings between now and the concert, and probably several phone calls. Being around Ella hurt, and he avoided her when he could. "Fine." How could he resist those tears? "But you have to promise me you'll never bring up the Muriel incident again."

Her mouth dropped open and snapped shut. "Okay." The response was uncharacteristically weak and lacking her usual fire. She seemed...broken.

He handed her a tissue from the box on his desk. "Here. Let me see that list."

She rummaged in her red leather bag and handed him a small stack of neatly folded papers. "Thank you," she whispered.

·♥·♥·♥·♥·♥·

Chapter Two

T he papers trembled as Ella held them out to him. She couldn't believe he'd agreed to work with her. She couldn't believe she'd confessed her fears. He'd always had the ability to make her open her heart. They'd been neighbors from the time his family moved to town until she went away to university. Even after their breakup, she was susceptible to his charms.

When she came back to Berry Cove after university and went to work at the school, she moved into a bachelor's apartment and had stayed there. Her friends teased her about the small space, but it was cozy and welcoming, and all she needed. Someday, she'd use the money she was saving to pay cash for a house. A house far away from him.

She studied him as he flipped through the list. His brows rose as he turned the page. He lifted his beautiful cocoa brown eyes to hers and scraped his hand through his black hair, making it stand on end.

"Is this for real? A thousand biscotti?"

"We're raising money for new playground equipment. The entire event is a fundraiser. There's a small entry fee. You can sit on Santa's lap for free, if we find a Santa, and for a couple extra bucks, get professional digital pictures. There's a carnival with games, a bake sale, and a cake walk."

"What's a cake walk?"

"Parents donate cakes. You place secret bids. The highest bidder gets to walk down the cake line and choose a cake to take home. Then the next bid...on and on down to the lowest bid."

"That sounds like fun. I can donate a cake to that. Something fancy."

"We-I, would appreciate that."

"Anything for you, Ella. Leave this list with me and I'll work up a quote by the middle of next week."

"Um. I need it by Monday. If I don't turn it in Tuesday..."

"Son of a.... Fine. I'll do it tonight. Something has to be done about that man. It's only October. Halloween is next week. Why does he need a budget now?"

"I have no idea. If it didn't make me sound paranoid, I'd say to spite me. I really appreciate you doing this for me, especially with our history."

He shook his finger. Again. "Uh uh. No talking about the past."

She rolled her eyes. "Fine." She didn't want to let it go. He'd hurt her. Badly. She bit her tongue to keep her pain from bursting out into words. She needed him to work with her, to keep her job.

"Meet me for breakfast tomorrow morning. Eight a.m. at Ruby's. I can already see that I'll have questions. We can hash out details over some corned beef hash."

"I haven't had that in ages. I didn't realize Ruby's even served it."

"New menu. I went last week with Murray, Neil, Jarod, Max, and Mark. We get together to shoot the breeze every couple of weeks. Sometimes at the bar, sometimes for brekky. Usually, when you gals get together."

She had no idea what to say to that. Her friends hadn't mentioned where their guys went. Probably because they knew she had no interest in what Vince was up to. Small-town life was tough in that everyone knew all about everyone else. But the blessing of good friends who wanted to protect her couldn't be beat.

"So? Can I buy you breakfast?"

"I'll meet you for breakfast. To discuss the list. But I'm paying for my own."

His expression morphed into a jaw-splitting grin. "I can live with that. Let me grab your latte. You can finish it in here while I finish this list."

Finish it? She hadn't even started it.

Still, she wasn't eager to go back out into the cold night air. It was toasty and warm here in his office. And it smelled deliciously of coffee and baked goods. Nothing beat the smell of a bakery. She slipped out of her long wool coat, tucked her earmuffs, mitts, and scarf into the sleeve, and leaned back in the chair.

She hadn't been in his office for a decade. She'd last been here when it was his mother's office. It hadn't changed much, though there was now a laptop where a rack of handwritten recipe books used to stand on the desk. The books had been moved to a new bookcase. Most of the shelves held kitchen gadgets and family photos. She rose to look at them.

His parents' wedding picture looked historic in black and white. Baby pictures of Vince, his brother Leo, and his sister Amelia. Family Christmas pictures taken through the years. She picked up a recent one, one without his father, to look at it more closely. When she went to set it back, she bumped a picture that was behind it.

She froze and stared at the picture in the handcrafted wooden frame. She'd made that frame in Industrial Arts class. After metalworking, pottery, and welding, she'd learned basic woodworking. She could already cook, so she'd skipped Cooking in favor of Industrial Arts. Inside the frame was a picture of her and Vince at the beach.

Lord, they'd changed so much since then. They were both taller, and they'd filled out. Sometime over the years, they'd both gotten a few lines around their eyes. They were still young, both of them thirty-six. But they sure weren't the innocent kids they had been in the photo.

"Snooping?"

She whirled around, nearly dropping the picture in her hand. "Yup." There was no sense trying to deny it. "I can't believe you still have this."

"Of course I do. It was a gift. From you."

"Are you saying you kept the gifts I gave you?"

"Of course I did. Didn't you?"

"Nope. Donated them all to the thrift store," she lied, hoping he didn't see the heat in her cheeks. She'd kept every damned one of them in a locked box in her closet. Not locked to keep others out, but locked to keep herself from getting in easily, and to keep her from falling into the past and wishing it was the present. She put the pictures back and returned to her chair.

Disappointment slid over his features as he carefully placed her latte and biscotti onto the table. "Here you go. Enjoy." He picked up her list off the table and slid into his chair behind the battered wooden desk.

With his attention on the list, she was able to study him. His hair was cropped short, much shorter than it had been when they dated. It was sexily mussed from when he'd run his fingers through it. Her fingers itched to touch his dark five-o'clock shadow, and the breadth of his shoulders practically begged to be hugged.

Ya. He was still hot. Probably hotter now than he'd been back then. A huge part of her had wished she'd been brave enough to give in to his easy pressure to sleep with him. At least she'd know what it would have been like. She sighed for the missed opportunity.

"You're staring," he said without looking up.

"Sorry."

"It's okay. I know I'm irresistible."

"Ha. Ha. Very funny."

"You always liked my sense of humor."

"You do have a gift for bad puns."

"I'm very punny."

A small laugh burst out of her. She clapped her hand over her mouth.

"You never could resist laughing over that one." His grin was pure rogue.

"And on that note, I'm going to get the girl out front to put this into a takeout cup for me."

"If you wait twenty minutes, I'll drive you home. It's on my way. I noticed that you walked here. The temperature is dropping. You might as well ride home in comfort."

"In a cold car."

"Nope. In my new SUV. Heated seats and command start. It'll be like a warming oven. Toasty and perfect."

"You got rid of the Mustang?"

"Naw. She's a classic. She's in the garage alongside my '72 GMC pickup and a '79 Chevelle Super Sport. I'll never give up my classics."

"You have a three-car garage?" When had he gotten that, and how had it slipped past her radar?

"Actually," his cheeks turned pink, and he avoided her eyes. "I have two five-car garages. I sort of won the lottery with a ticket Mom gave me for Christmas a couple of years ago. I purchased that big house out on Lakeshore Road. Not for the house, but for the garages." His shrug was eloquent.

"And you still work?"

"I do. I love this place. It gives me purpose. The lotto money lets me pamper my family and friends, and gives me security for my retirement, though I can't see myself retiring until I'm much older. Baking is who I am."

"I'm impressed." She laughed. "And here you were grumbling about a big order."

"I'm set for life, but I'm not stupid enough to want to virtually give away my efforts." He grinned. "But I will tell you you'll get a better deal than I ever gave Muriel."

"I appreciate that." She sipped her coffee and watched him type the order into his computer. "I don't know why he didn't email that over," she said.

"Muriel was partial to delivering the list in person. She's been the liaison for the past four years. Is she going to be mad at you?"

Ella shrugged. "Probably. But she's not exactly my friend anyway, and I didn't arrange this. Brewer did."

A few minutes later, she swallowed the last of her drink just as Vince stood up.

"Are you ready to go, Ella?"

"Absolutely. Just let me take my cup out."

"Just put it in the kitchen sink. The staff have all clocked out and gone."

"How do you know that?"

"The time sheets are uploaded and record when someone clocks in or out. It's all on the computer. And Amy waved as she walked by on her way out. Give me two minutes to confirm that the front is locked and the machines are powered down, and we can go. I started the car a couple minutes ago. It's out back, warmed and waiting."

It felt like no time until they were in his heated SUV.

"You should come out and see my place sometime," Vince said, though he kept his eyes on the road.

There was a ton of snow falling, and it was piling up quickly. She hoped his new SUV had great tires. "Why would I do that?"

He shrugged. "I'm...just curious as to whether or not you'll like it. It has an indoor resistance pool."

"Oh. I would like that. I still swim three times a week." She'd been on the high school swim team. She wasn't the best, but she was darn close and had won a few long-distance swim races.

"I can tell that you still work out." He slowed to a stop outside her building. "Here you go. Do you want me to pick you up tomorrow?"

"Thanks, but no. It's supposed to be warm. I'll meet you there." He sat in the vehicle waiting as she walked up the sidewalk and let herself inside. His patience and unspoken concern for her safety warmed her almost as much as knowing that he still liked the way she looked.

·♥·♥·♥·♥·♥·

Chapter Three

V ince sat in the back corner of Ruby's, waiting for Ella. Ruby's
was a modern restaurant with an old-fashioned feel. Pale blue
walls were decorated with black and white photographs of the Berry
Cove area. The seats were well-padded and comfortable with plenty
of room between them.

The chimes rang as someone entered, and he looked up from the
Dwayne Clayden thriller he was reading and wished he hadn't.

Muriel.

Her smile was bright as she hurried over to him. He used a paper
napkin to mark his page and closed the book.

"Vince. So good to see you."

"Muriel." Maybe if he was curt enough, she'd go away. *Nope.* She
slid into the booth across from him.

"Mind if I join you for breakfast?" She unzipped her jacket.

"Actually, yes, I do mind. I'm meeting someone."

Her brows pinched together. "Oh? Who?" Her smile was pure
flirtation. She was beautiful, but she did nothing for him. Mint
wafted across the table. At least she no longer smelled like stale
coffee.

"Not that it's any of your business, but I'm meeting Ella."

"Ella Ryan? Gabriella Ryan?" Her frown fled, and deep grooves marred her forehead. "She has no interest in you. I, on the other hand...." she trailed off suggestively and reached out to caress his hand.

He jerked away from her. The last thing he needed was for Ella to see them together. Touching would be the straw that broke the camel's back. He had to get rid of Muriel if he had any hope of rekindling his long-dead relationship with Ella.

"Yes. Gabriella Ryan. Now, if you don't mind. I'd like you to leave before she arrives."

"But Vince...you and I could be really good together." There was desperation in her voice.

He withheld a wince. He felt for her loneliness. He really did. But his heart was stuck on Ella. He'd dated half a dozen women when he was in university, and three since he came back to Berry Cove. None of them, not a single one, moved his heart like Ella had. Like she still did.

"Muriel. I've turned you down hundreds, if not thousands, of times. You're a nice woman. But you aren't the woman for me. Somewhere, out there," he waved toward the door, "is a man who will love you with all his heart. Unfortunately for you, it isn't me."

"What's she got that I don't have?" She gestured wildly and slapped her palm on the table, making half the patrons of Ruby's turn in their direction.

"It isn't anything I can put my finger on. Honestly, I've tried. My Gramma Beth always said, "The heart wants what the heart wants. No sense trying to force love, because that way leads to madness." I believe she's right. My heart wants Ella. For better or worse. I won't settle. I'd rather die alone than force something and end up hurting another person. That includes you. You deserve better." The disappointment on her face cut deep into his chest. Nobody deserved to be slapped down the way he'd just had to do, but he was at his wits' end.

He inhaled a steadying breath. "I'm sorry if I hurt you. Maybe if I had never met Ella..." He didn't finish the thought. He didn't want to get her hopes up after hopefully getting his point across.

"Fine." She jumped up from the table and glared down at him. "Someday, you'll wish you'd chosen me."

He couldn't decide if the words were supposed to be a threat or a wild hope on her part.

"Goodbye, Muriel. I wish you well."

She whirled on her heel and fled, nearly plowing into a server in her haste.

He should have been relieved, but knowing he'd hurt her left him with an unsettled feeling. At least until Ella walked in a few seconds later. She paused in the doorway to unbutton her coat; her eyes scanned the room and paused when she noticed him. A brief smile flickered on her luscious lips before she turned serious again. Large snowflakes glittered in her bright red hair and on the shoulders of her navy coat.

She wiped her boots and started toward him, stopping to talk to several people on her way. A young boy, probably one of her students, raced up to her and hugged her. Lifting her long coat so it didn't rub on the floor, she squatted down and talked to him. After a moment, she hugged him and stood. The boy looked like he'd won the lottery, and his parents smiled at her.

Vince bit back his own smile. She had such a lovely, outgoing personality; was it any wonder that he found her irresistible?

"Good morning, Ella." He stood when she got to the table. "Can I take your coat?"

She blushed. "Thank you." She turned around, and he helped her slide the coat off and hung it from the hook on the end of her bench.

He poured her a coffee from their carafe as she slid into her seat. "You look lovely. That fuchsia looks great on you." He gestured toward her bulky sweater.

"Even with my red hair?" Her cheeks turned pink.

Good, she wasn't totally immune to him.

"Even with your red hair," he agreed, pushing the bowl of creamers her way.

"Thanks. Did I just see Muriel leave?" Her tone was flat.

He sighed. "Yes, you did. She stopped in and sat with me." Before Ella could respond, he went on, "I told her, in no uncertain terms, that I was not interested and never will be. I feel awful. She was really upset." He sipped his coffee, trying to swallow the bad feeling along with the caffeine. "I've been subtle. I've been kind. I've avoided her. This morning, I resorted to cold brutality."

Ella reached out and patted his hand, much like Muriel had done. Only this time it felt right.

"That must have been difficult. You're not the type of man to hurt someone needlessly." She poured three creamers into her coffee, stirred it, and picked up the white earthenware mug. She cradled it in her hands for several seconds before sipping cautiously. "Oh, this is good. First cup of the day."

"You always did love your coffee, even in tenth grade."

"Much to Mom's dismay." They laughed together. When the laughter faded to smiles, she said, "Shall we get into the school's order?"

"I thought we could eat first. Maybe catch up." Not that he wasn't totally up to date on her life. Their mothers were friends and still got together frequently.

Uncertainty passed over her face. She frowned. Then nodded slowly. "I guess that's okay."

"I'll go first." He waggled his brows in the manner that always made her laugh. A light chuckle was his reward. "I've just got this huge order for my business. Well," he corrected, "a quote request at least. It's for a charity event. I'm thinking my profit will only be fifteen cents per item. That's over ingredient cost and doesn't include the extra manpower I'll need to create it all."

"You don't have to do that," she objected.

"I know I don't. I want to. I went by the school playground this morning. It's abysmal. I want the kids to have the best equipment. My kids will attend that school someday."

"You're dating?" She blinked rapidly. "I...I didn't know that."

"No. I'm not. But there's a woman I'd like to ask out. But she avoids me at every turn." He was taking a risk. Putting himself on the line. Hopefully, Ella wouldn't be scared off.

"She's an idiot if she's avoiding you. You're a great guy, Vince. Even without your lottery money."

"Shsh." He glanced around. "Nobody knows. I managed to keep it a secret. I don't want people coming out of the woodwork looking for their share. I give generously to a dozen charities. Particularly the Alberta Children's Hospital and the Stollery Children's Hospital."

"That's fabulous. Tell me about this woman." She asked the question, but her tone was pure disinterest.

·♥·♥·♥·♥·♥·

E lla held back a frown. *He was dating?*

"She lives in town. She's kind, generous, pretty, and smart." He smiled like a man in love, and her heart dipped to her toes.

Ridiculous, because she didn't want him.

"She's a teacher, and not Muriel."

"Hey, can I take your order?" Ella was never so glad to be interrupted by a server.

"Yes!" She scanned the menu. "I'll have the corned beef hash breakfast platter, please. Make my eggs over easy."

"Make that two," Vince added.

"Sure thing. And Vince, the boss says thanks for the desserts you just brought in. He's good for the weekend."

"Tell him he's very welcome."

The young woman nodded and strolled away.

"Desserts?" Ella asked, grasping for any change of subject.

"I provide the desserts for Ruby's and for a couple other restaurants in town."

"How did I not know that?" Her mother talked about him constantly. Just last week, she'd lamented on the fact that the two of them weren't still in a relationship.

He shrugged. "We're not in the same circle. Anyway, I'm hoping this girl will go to tomorrow's high school football game with me. It's the playoffs."

"Oh." She wrinkled her nose. She wasn't a huge football fan, but the idea of Vince taking another woman sat heavily on her stomach. Maybe she should have skipped the heavy corned beef breakfast in favor of plain toast.

"So, will you go with me?"

She blinked. "What?" *Wasn't he interested in someone else?*

"Will you go to the football game with me tomorrow afternoon?"

"In the snow? What about the woman you want to date? Aren't you going to ruin your chances with her?"

He raised one eyebrow and didn't say anything. He just looked at her. For one minute. Then another. Finally, after an embarrassingly long amount of time, it dawned on her that Vince wanted to date her.

"What? Why?" She stammered, looking for clarity. "You want to date me?"

"Yes, Gabriella Ryan, I want to date you."

"Been there, done that."

"And you've got the T-shirt too," he added. "At least you did have, from that Allan Jackson concert we attended."

She still had it. Hers, and his. When she was particularly down in the dumps, she slept in his, wishing it still smelled like him. For all that logic told her he was one hundred percent wrong for her, her heart refused to listen to her brain.

"Think about it, Ella. If we didn't have an ugly history between us. If you just met me today. If I asked you out, what would you say? I'm a decent looking guy. I run a successful business. I've got strong family and community ties. I go to church. I'm good to my mom." He waited for twenty seconds and said, "If we had just met, would you go out with me?"

He wasn't wrong. He was all those things. And more. And if he hadn't broken her heart, he would have been just the type of guy she was looking for. She couldn't lie to him, but she also couldn't agree. So, she shook her head. At least it wasn't a verbal lie.

"I don't believe you." His words were barely more than a whisper. "I think you and I would meet, we'd like each other, we'd date...and who knows where that would go."

She shook her head, negating the idea.

"Why not give it a shot? I'm not the idiot I was in high school. I've matured. I've learned the value of a good woman, of a serious relationship. Of you. I still love you, Gabriella." After a long pause, he added, "And Muriel sure as hell won't get close enough to kiss me."

"I thought we weren't talking about that?"

"After everything I've said, that's what you hone in on? Incredible." He pulled a folder from the bench beside him and slapped it on the table. "Here's your quote." He stood and yanked his jacket on. "I'll be at the game. After church. Placker Field. Tomorrow at two. Your ticket will be at the gate. Join me or not. I'm tired of wishing and hoping. Either you show up tomorrow, and we try to see what we could be together, or there's a bakery in Rimbey that's up for sale. Seems like Rimbey would be a great place for me to relocate to."

She pivoted in her seat to watch him go, her knuckles and fingertips white where she gripped the table to keep from going after him.

"Girl, that was a huge mistake."

"What?" She spun further around to stare at the elderly woman in the next booth. "Mrs. Cooper. I didn't see you there."

"Go after him," the septuagenarian ordered. "That's one good man, and he's been gone on you for years. He used to follow you everywhere. He doesn't even date any longer."

"Um." She blinked at the former high school principal. "He's not for me."

"Only because you're stubbornly holding a mistake against him. We all make mistakes, dear. Some are bigger than others. How would you feel if someone refused to forgive you for a small mistake?"

·❤·❤·❤·❤·❤·

Chapter Four

The crowd stood and roared as the Berry Cove Titans raced onto the field to meet their opponents, the Falkville Falcons. Vince didn't join them. He sat in his seat, defeated. Giving Ella an ultimatum was an idiotic move. Now, he'd have to leave the town he loved and move to Rimbey, or somewhere else where he could ply his trade as a baker.

He should have known better. Ella was stubborn. Really stubborn. He should have gone with subtlety. Snuck in under her radar. Didn't they do that in those ridiculous romance movies she loved so much? Hang around, do small things, be there for the heroine? Steal her heart while she wasn't expecting it?

He banked a sigh and clapped lamely. He had been excited for this game, but he'd messed up with the ultimatum. Maybe she was right. He wasn't good enough for her.

He listened to the game preamble, trying not to focus on the empty seat beside him. The ticket office would close soon. He stood and muttered the national anthem along with the crowd. *Would this be the last time he sang it in Berry Cove?*

How was he going to leave his mom? His friends? His customers? At times like this, he wished he could cuss a blue streak. Dang and heck just didn't seem adequate to express his irritation at himself.

The cheer squad did their thing, and the game began. He tried to focus. This game was crucial for the team, and some of his friends had kids on the team. He wanted them to win. His gaze kept straying to the stairs leading up to his seat.

Hoping.

When the whistle blew to start the second quarter, he knew she wasn't coming.

·♥ · ♥ · ♥ · ♥ · ♥·

E lla huddled in the corner of the concourse during the intermission, staying clear of the crowd and hoping she didn't run into any of her friends. She was here, and for the life of her, she didn't know why.

When the whistle blew to start the second quarter game play, she knew it was now or never. She either had to go into the stands to find Vince or she had to leave and cut him out of her life.

Forever.

She didn't want to date him. But she couldn't stand the thought of losing him either. Besides, if he left, his mother would miss him. Or she'd go with him, and her mother would lose her best friend. She couldn't allow that.

She shushed the voice telling her to stop making excuses. She was here because she cared for him.

Slowly, with unease dragging heavy on her feet, she trudged from the concourse and climbed the stairs toward her seat.

Vince was chatting to the man beside him, and she got halfway up the stairs before he turned her way. He paused midmotion, reared back slightly, and his jaw dropped open like he couldn't believe she'd arrived. Then, he smiled.

Oh lord, that smile. It warmed her icy fingers and toes. Her heart went pitapat. Her head went light, and she stumbled. He was out of his seat in a second. He flew down the stairs and grasped her elbow.

"Hey. Are you okay?"

"Ya," she said breathlessly. "I am." Way better than she should be, but she'd keep that tidbit to herself. "I just...I just caught my toe." She was not struck blind by his amazing smile and the pure happiness in his eyes.

"Come on. Let me help you to your seat."

Obediently, she let him lead her upward and past the three people occupying the end seats.

"Hold up a second." He reached past her and picked up a cardboard drink tray. "There you go. Take a seat."

She slid into the furthest seat. It was still warm from where he'd been sitting. She snuggled into the warmth. "Thanks."

"This is for you." He passed her the tray. "It was hot chocolate. It's probably not that warm now." He shrugged. "And a chocolate croissant. I missed you at church this morning."

Her cheeks heated. She'd been there. She snuck in the back late and scurried out before the service ended. She'd spent the rest of the morning trying to find reasons not to come to the game. "I was...late."

He raised one eyebrow.

Dang it. He knew she was lying.

"What's the score?" She didn't care one fig about the game. She was just stupidly happy to sit beside Vince.

"Seventeen-ten. For us." He leaned close and whispered, "I'm glad you came." His breath tickled her ear.

"I came because Berry Cove, and your mom need you."

He quirked that eyebrow again. The crowd cheered, and she jumped up with everyone else to root for the team, though she had no idea what was going on.

She sat back, trying not to lean into the arm he'd slung across the back of her seat.

Eventually, she was able to focus on the game and not his presence or his body heat. She even managed to ignore the voice telling her this was exactly where she belonged.

·♥·♥·♥·♥·♥·

"You guys coming to the pub with us?" Jacinda asked when they ran into her and Murray on their way out after the team's victory.

Vince looked down at her. "That's up to Ella. I'm not sure what her plans are."

Ella squirmed under his gaze. If she went, she was admitting he was part of her life again. Maybe not in a relationship, but at least as a friend. Confusion rolled in her mind, and her stomach was heavy with unresolved feelings.

"Come on, Ella. Please." Jacinda drew the plea into three long syllables. "We haven't been out as a group in for-ev-er."

The crowd swirled around them while she debated with herself.

"I'm buying," Murray added as if the cost mattered.

"Well, in that case, I'm in." She grasped at cost as an excuse to set aside her reluctance. Something stilled within her...as if she'd made the right decision.

Despite the fact that the game was between two high school teams, the pub was rocking with their victory. The local team, their classmates, and their parents would be celebrating at a nearby pizzeria. But the bar was partying as well.

"About time you got here," Julia declared. She sat with her husband, Neil. She gave Ella a questioning look.

Ella shrugged it off. There would be questions later for sure.

"Took me a while to get Ella to come along. She kept grumbling about having marking to do," Vince said.

"I wanted to get it done before the Halloween party on Monday. I know I won't have the energy for marking after the kid's celebration. They were already wild on Friday."

"I don't envy you that." Vince pulled a chair out and gestured for her to sit beside Julia. He took the seat beside Ella after she sat. All their friends crowded around the table after vying for seating. "How'd you snag such a big table?"

Julia laughed. "I'm the mayor. I booked it in advance. Grabbing a table is one of the few unofficial perks I take advantage of."

"I've always respected that about you," Ella said. "Your honesty is part of your character."

The server interrupted the conversation and took their orders. When Vince was distracted by his friend Max, Julia leaned in and whispered, "I can't believe you're here with Vince, Ella. What's going on?"

Ella stole a glance to be sure Vince wasn't listening. "I don't know. He asked. I went." She tried to shrug the question off, and judging by the look on Julia's face, she failed.

"I'm totally phoning you later and you will spill the tea." Fortunately, she dropped the subject, and Ella relaxed into the comfortable joy of being with old friends.

Chapter Five

E lla stared down at her cell phone.

Vince: Want to grab dinner after work?

More than anything! But her heart kept trying to keep him away.

Ella: Maybe? What are you thinking?

Vince: Food. Whatever you want. There's a new Polish place downtown.

Ella: I've never tried Polish.

Vince: You'll love it.

Three dots appeared, disappeared, and reappeared. He was texting her again and saving her from making an immediate decision.

Vince: Please.

They'd been out with their friends three times during November. Not dates exactly. Group events, though he'd picked her up and brought her home. Each time, she fell deeper under his spell.

Ella: Who else is going?

Vince: Just us.

Ella: Like a date??

She added a confused emoji.

Vince: Only if you want it to be.

That was the crux of the entire debacle. She wanted it to be. They were compatible in so many ways. They shared a church and their faith. They believed in strong family values. They both worked hard and cared about their friends. If he were any other man, she'd be deeply in love with him and waiting for him to propose.

Ella: Friends only. Not a date.

Vince: As you wish.

Dang it. He knew darn well those three words would make her think of *The Princess Bride*. She huffed out a confused and frustrated breath.

Ella: Pick me up at seven.

Her crazy heart did a happy dance, and she hummed all afternoon while she cleaned her tiny apartment and worked on a beaded bracelet. Crafting usually gave her stability. Today, her thoughts kept turning to what Vince would think of the project. He'd always been super supportive when she created things while they were dating.

"Stop it. You aren't dating. He's a friend."

The sweet and annoying voice in the back of her mind whispered that they could be more. She could finally let go and love again...if she wanted to.

"No. I'm not certain of him. He has to prove himself."

She'd had exactly that argument with Julia when she called the night of the football game. Julia had disagreed.

"Why are you being so stubborn?" Julia demanded. "Even as you tell it, he didn't kiss Muriel. He's done nothing wrong. Even if he had, that was years ago. He's not the boy he was back then. Jeepers, Ella. He hasn't dated in as long as I can remember. He's waiting for you."

"I'm scared." The confession snuck out before she could stop it.

Her friend's last advice before she hung up was, "We're all afraid of something, Ella. Don't let fear hold you back from what could be the love of your life."

Irritated at the memory, she dropped her tools onto her tiny table and stood. Pacing the small confines of her bachelor apartment, she fought with herself. An hour later, after a long walk outside, she still hadn't calmed down.

·♥·♥·♥·♥·♥·

Vince's hand was gentle on the small of her back as he led Ella into Iza's Deli. She tried to distance herself, but as she sped up, he kept pace. There was no escaping him.

She paused inside the door to look around. Iza's had the classic deli look, but upgraded a bit, making it suitable for a nice evening out. Not fancy, but not plain either. Paintings of Poland were sprinkled around the walls. Dark chairs sat in front of tan tables. The air smelled incredibly of meat and spices, with just a hint of sauerkraut. Her stomach growled.

"I guess we got here just in time." His laugh danced along her skin, making her shiver in delight.

Lord have mercy, he had the best laugh.

"I guess so."

They took a seat near the window and discussed food options. Dinner was filled with easy conversation about their families and politics. They disagreed on books and movies. He leaned toward mystery and action. She adored anything romantic. Perhaps that was why she needed proof that he was different now. Logically, she knew he would be. After all, she wasn't the same girl she'd been back then. She'd grown and matured. Maybe he was worth taking a risk on.

Still, that tiny kernel of doubt wouldn't be silenced.

"Heads up," Vince muttered.

"What?"

"Muriel's headed this way."

Why now? Why, when she was just warming to him? Ella braced herself for conflict.

Muriel slid into the seat beside Vince.

"Ella," she declared, "I'm glad I saw you. You won't believe the father of your new student. Oh my gosh, he's the handsomest man

I've ever met. He's just so...dreamy." Her eyes took on a faraway look. She blinked and turned toward Vince. "Sorry, Vince. I don't know what I was thinking. You definitely aren't the man for me. Thank heaven you weren't interested."

"Um, thanks?" He shook his head in bewilderment.

"Ella, should I date him?"

"Him who?"

"Your student's father. He asked me to dinner."

"There's no rule against it," Ella said, still half confused.

"Awesome. I'm going to say yes." She leaped up and took two steps away before rushing back. "Ella, I owe you an apology." She hung her head. "Vince never kissed me. I kissed him. I wanted him for my own. I'm sorry I ruined what you had." She waggled her fingers and took off across the deli and out the door.

Ella sat in stunned silence. Vince looked thunderstruck.

"Wow," she murmured after several minutes. He'd been telling the truth. She had years of anger and upset to reconsider. It wasn't going to be easy to get over that bombshell.

"Um. Dessert?" Vince asked. "I hear the apple cake here is divine."

"Sure." Her knees were shaking from Muriel's statements. There was no way Ella was walking out of here until she calmed down and got a grip on her whirling emotions.

They ate dessert and lingered over decaf coffee.

"I'm going to ask you something, and I don't want an answer tonight. Okay?"

"Okay?" His question surprised her and made her uneasy. She twisted her cloth napkin between her hands until she thought it might tear under the strain.

"Ella, considering what just happened, would you consider going on an *actual* date with me? Not a friend's dinner. Not a group date with our mutual friends. An actual date. One man, one woman; getting to know each other and seeing if there is potential for the future between us."

She opened her mouth to reply.

"Not now. Think about it. No ultimatum this time. No threats. No begging. Just consider the idea and get back to me in a few days. Okay?"

Slowly, with deliberate motions, she ate the last few bites of her cake and sipped the last of her coffee. "Vince," she began, and set down her fork to pick up her napkin.

His shoulders went tense, and worry filled his eyes. His lips pressed together.

"Vince, I would be happy to go on a date with you." She kept her voice calm and as even as she could, but she was shivering with excitement at seeing where this would go now that she knew the truth. If that made her fickle...so be it.

Yes, she should have trusted him enough to believe him, but she'd been an insecure child and not ready for a mature relationship. Maybe now they'd find what they could have had if she'd been different.

"Oh, thank God." He reached across the table and clasped her hands in his, stilling her motion of twisting the napkin. "I was scared spitless you'd say no."

·❤·❤·❤·❤·❤·

Chapter Six

Ella looked around the school gym. The parents' decorating committee had done an incredible job. Fairy lights hung from the roof and walls. A ten-foot tree glowed in each corner of the gym. Glow-in-the-dark stars shone on the walls and floor. The gym was a Christmas wonderland and the most romantic place she'd ever seen. *Silent Night* played over the speakers.

Earlier, an amazing Santa with sparkling eyes and a red velvet suit had wandered through the crowd, talking to everyone. She still hadn't figured out who it had been, but he'd encouraged her to follow her heart and let the spirit of Christmas set her free.

The entire event had been thrust onto her when Principal Brewer had suddenly retired. She was still on edge, worrying, but for now, the post-concert celebration was going perfectly.

Hundreds of people, not just students and parents of the school, had come out for the cake walk, food sale, and dance. The concert was held during the last hour of school. The fundraiser began at six-thirty and was nearing its end. Hot dog sales had been out of this world. The cake walk had been a resounding success.

Couples and family groups danced together to the DJ's music. Others lingered around the edges of the dance floor, talking and laughing. Her heart was full with the event's success. She hadn't taken the time to count the funds they'd brought in...there was still a brimming cash donation box to deal with in addition to everything else they'd collected, but if she was any judge, they'd have more than enough money for an entirely new playground. Probably for one much larger than the old structures.

Vince strode through the crowd toward her and swept her into his arms. He bussed a discreet kiss on her cheek. "Come, dance with me. The DJ says this is the final song."

As if on cue, the music morphed into a slow waltz and one of her favorite classic country songs. She smiled her agreement and let him lead her onto to dance floor.

They still fit together as well as they did as teens. She rested her head on his chest and listened to the low thumping of his heart. She was filled with a total sense of rightness. This was where she was meant to be. Forever.

"Vince?"

"Hm?"

"Can I ask you something?"

"Sure. After the dance. I don't want to miss a moment of holding you close."

He'd said that every time they'd danced at the pub. And every night when he'd dropped her home after their many dates since their Polish dinner. Each time he whispered the words, her heart fell harder. Finally, the music ended, and people began streaming from the school gym.

"Vince?"

"Ella?"

"Be serious, Vince."

He nodded and met her gaze fully in the still-dim lights.

"Vince, I was a fool. I was wrong. I apologize for jumping the gun and believing the worst of you. I've seen my mistake, and I promise not to repeat it."

He kept looking at her, questions in his eyes, but he nodded.

"Vince, will you forgive me? Will you marry me?"

He whooped out loud. "Heck yes!"

He spun her round and round in wild circles before shouting, "I said yes! We're getting married."

Their friends, still standing on the sidelines, cheered and rushed over to congratulate them.

"Ella," he whispered, his lips a hair's breadth from hers, "I promise you'll never regret asking me."

About Katie

Alberta romance author Katie O'Connor can't live without her computer and eReader, and her favorite place to use them is in the woods while watching the deer frolic on her summer property, Sanctuary.

Her passion, aside from romance and her grandbabies, is giving back to the writing community. She's always eager to share what she's learned about writing and romance. In 2025, she was a Story Coach in the Alexandra Writers' Centre's Author Development Program. She is also a writing coach and happy to help new authors with their work.

She's fueled by coffee and steak, and is fluent in sarcasm, cussing, dad jokes, and romantic jargon. If you need her, she'll be cozied up by the coffee pot, eyeing the cookies.

Where to Find Katie

Website:
https://katieohwrites.com
Email:
katie@katieohwrites.com
Newsletter Signup:
http://eepurl.com/Q2nRr
Facebook:
http://www.facebook.com/katieohwrites
Bookbub:
https://www.bookbub.com/profile/katie-o-connor

Instagram:
https://www.instagram.com/katieohwrites/

Goodreads:

https://www.goodreads.com/author/show/5362469.Katie_O_Connor

Other Books by Katie

Coyote Creek:
A Lesson in Love 1
A Heart Torn Apart 2
A Secret to Shatter 3
A Melody for Christmas 4
A Surrender so Sweet 5
A Place Called Home 6
A Love to Rebuild 7
Coming Home for Christmas 8
Coyote Creek Box Set 1
Coyote Creek Box Set 2
Cherry Lake Fire Fighters:
Sugar Cookie Kisses
Cappuccino Mugs and Fire Fighter Hugs
A Silver Fox Christmas:
Their Christmas Heart
Their Christmas Love
Their Perfect Christmas
A Silver Fox Christmas Box Set
Heart's Haven:
Running Home

Building Trust
Saving Grace
Loving Winter
Heart's Haven Box Set
Three Moon Falls:
Fire Magic
Water Magic
Earth Magic
Midnight Magic
Air Magic
Stand-Alone Books:
Carly's Heart
Matchmaker Christmas
Cupid's Charm
Gingerbread Dreams
Christmas in Silver Creek
Fake Dating at Half Moon Bay
Playing for Keeps in Half Moon Bay
Sleigh Bells Inn
Hearts in the Spotlight
To a Tea
Bulletproof Heart
Protecting Josie
Rekindled Fire
Winning Her Love
Ticket to Her Heart
KO'd by Love
Christmas in Berry Cove